RADICAL RAG

THE PIONEER LABOUR PRESS IN CANADA

Ron Verzuh

FOREWORD BY ED FINN

Canadian Cataloguing in Publication Data

Verzuh, Ron, 1948—
    Radical Rag: The Pioneer Labour Press in Canada

Includes index.
Bibliography: p.
ISBN 0-88791-039-4

1. Press, Labour—Canada—History—19th century.   2. Labor and laboring classes—Canada—History—19th century.   I. Title.

PN4914.L3V47 1988   070.4′493318′0971   C89-090030-2

Cover design: Kris Klaasen, Vancouver
Printing by Mutual Press, Ottawa

This book has been published with assistance from the Canada Council and the Ontario Arts Council. We also wish to acknowledge the Summer Employment/Experience Development programme of Employment and Immigration Canada.

ISBN 0-88791-039-4

Steel Rail Publishing, Ottawa

Contents

Not sure

Acknowledgements

I owe debts of gratitude to many people who helped me during the writing of this book. First and foremost is my wife Valerie Raymond, who is my first and best editor. The staffs of the National Library of Canada, Danny Moore in particular, and the Canada Labour Library, Fred Longley in particular, were most helpful. I must also thank librarians in special collections sections and city libraries around the country. I am indebted to the Institute of Canadian Studies at Carleton University and thesis adviser Bob Rupert for providing expert criticism while I prepared the masters thesis on which this book is based. I must also thank Terry Binnersley at Steel Rail Publishing and researcher Allison Webb for helping me turn the thesis into a book. The success of that enterprise must be shared with them. The failings are mine alone. Finally, I salute the editors of *Primary Sources in Canadian Working Class History*: Greg Kealey, Linda Kealey, Bryan Palmer and Russell Hann. As noted in *Primary Sources*, they took "the first step along the road to a more complete picture of the forgotten causes, the failed efforts, the obsolete skills, and the private strengths of the largely unknown men and women whose history is essential to an understanding of the world in which we live."

NOTE: Most pioneer labour papers used the "or" spelling for words such as labour. The notable exceptions were the *People's Magazine and Workingman's Guardian* and the *Trades Union Advocate*. For consistency, the "our" form and some other British spellings have been used throughout this book.

Foreword

Any popular movement, if it is to succeed, must be able to communicate with its prospective followers. The Canadian labour movement, in its struggling early years, relied heavily on the scores of working-class newspapers that sprang up all over the country in the late 1800s.

Launched mainly by reform-minded printers, these papers not only preached the benefits of unionization, but also attacked the evils of *laissez-faire* capitalism. They railed against child labour, poverty, slums, long hours of work, the exploitation of women, and all the other social ills that plagued working people in the days of the "robber barons."

It was the golden age of the labour press. The zealous and often eloquent labour editors filled their pages with colourfully written commentaries as well as informative news stories. They exposed onerous and unsafe working conditions and reported every improvement in those conditions that the unions were able to achieve.

The importance of the 19th-century labour press should not be exaggerated. The high illiteracy rate among workers at the time, as well as their inability to afford even the few cents it cost to buy a labour paper, limited circulation and readership. But there is no doubt that the papers were read by most union activists of the era, as well as by politicians and opinion-makers.

Indeed, without the pioneer labour press, the principles and policies of trade unionism would have been much more difficult to disseminate. So would the alternatives to private enterprise that the labour press ringingly espoused, ranging from the moderate reforms of the co-operative movement to the radical proposals of socialists and communists.

vi

Labour historians have tended to neglect or underestimate the role of the early labour papers. They are mentioned peripherally and sometimes quoted in labour histories, but no one until now has told their story in all its colour and diversity. *Radical Rag* fills that gap superbly. Ron Verzuh has mined a rich lode and produced a fascinating and readable account of the rise and fall of the labour press in Canada.

This is no dry academic tome. Lucidly written, spiced with anecdotes and sharp observations, it brings to life a gallery of crusty and committed labour journalists. Few union members today know anything about Eugene Donavon, Phillips Thompson, Joseph Marks, C.C. Steuart, George Wrigley, and the dozens of other labour writers and editors of the 1800s. Nor do the names of their papers — names such as the *Workingman's Journal*, the *Ontario Workman*, the *Trades Union Advocate*, the *Palladium of Labour*, the *Canada Labour Courier*, the *Labour Advocate*, the *Echo*, and the *People's Voice*—stir a responsive chord in today's unionists.

Some might even be inclined to question the relevance of those pioneers and their publications to the modern labour movement. But in fact we have a lot to learn from them. The objectives they pursued and the stands they took differ only in degree from those that today's unions still seek—free collective bargaining, the right to strike, more leisure time, pay equity, occupational health and safety and a higher minimum wage.

Progress has been made on all these fronts, but they still fall short of fulfillment. That's why the impassioned prose of the century-old labour papers often comes across with an uncannily modern ring. So much so that many of the words of a long-dead writer could be transplanted verbatim to the word processors in a union's public relations department today—and be just as topical and effective as they were a hundred years ago.

Radical Rag offers generous dollops of such quotes. But the book is much more than a sampling of the old labour press. It is a vivid chronicle of the life and times of the early labour movement's editorial champions. Verzuh does not glorify these advocacy journals or try to hide their shortcomings. They often feuded bitterly with one another and were guilty of shameful racist slurs against immigrant Chinese workers. Most of them were also given to male chauvinistic views about women in the work force.

Nevertheless, as Verzuh makes clear, on balance, and on most of the issues concerning the poor and the jobless as well as working people, the old-time editors and their papers took positions that flowed from a deep sense of social justice. They were motivated by a desire to make the economic system more equitable and humane. If they sometimes went astray, it was usually because of that strong and often emotional commitment.

The greatest value of this book is that it relates the author's study of the 19th-century labour press to the current reality of trade union public relations. He brings this perspective to bear in his preface and in the concluding chapter. Why, he wonders, did Canada have so many labour-supportive weekly newspapers a century ago and none today?

That question is raised in the context of a crucial distinction between the labour press and the union press. The journals that flourished in the golden age were published on behalf of workers and their unions, but they were often independently owned and operated. The publishers counted on unions for financial backing and subscriptions, but were not controlled by them. The papers were autonomous. Their editorial opinions almost always coincided with the aims and aspirations of union leaders, but not invariably. They were free to deviate from union policies and even to criticize them. This didn't happen often, but when it did it generated a lively and constructive debate. It also gave the labour papers more credibility than they would have enjoyed had they always slavishly parroted the official union line.

Today, instead of a labour press, we have a trade union press—hundreds of papers and magazines published by the unions for their members. They do a good job of boosting and defending the unions, but as house organs they do not reach beyond the union membership to the general public. Their value and influence are correspondingly diminished. It is left to the small-circulation magazines on the left — *Canadian Dimension*, *This Magazine* and *Our Times*, to name the most prominent—to print more analytical and objective articles sympathetic to labour. Such magazines, however, remain relatively few and all but inaccessible to most Canadians.

Perhaps Verzuh is being impractical when he proposes the rebirth of a labour press in this country. Conditions have changed drastically since the 1800s. Movies, television, organized sports events, and many other forms of entertainment compete for the worker's time. The costs of starting and sustaining a newspaper of any kind have risen astronomically. And today's labour leaders are much less disposed than their predecessors to fund a publication over which they do not exercise complete editorial power.

So the odds, as Verzuh himself concedes, are heavily weighted against the reflowering of a labour press akin to the one he so stirringly describes in this book. Whether a new golden age emerges or not, however, we are forcefully reminded in *Radical Rag* that it once existed and had its heyday and helped immeasurably to nurture and shape the labour movement as we know it today.

This book pays a long overdue tribute to the pioneer labour editors and their muckraking publications. Their slogans ring down through the decades: "Devoted to the interests of the producing classes!" "For the right against the wrong! For the weak against the strong!" Prose like that may seem flowery and pretentious to modern readers. But that was the accepted writing style in the Victorian era, and it moved and inspired many of the heroic reformers who were later to put their stamp on the political scene—people like Daniel J. O'Donoghue and J.S. Woodsworth.

Radical Rag captures all the rich flavour and nostalgia of the crusading labour journalists of the past, and shows the vital part they played in the birth and growth of Canada's labour movement.

Ed Finn
Editor, *The Facts*
Canadian Union of Public Employees

Preface

It is spring 1988 and the elite of today's labour editors are gathered for the Canadian Association of Labour Media awards in Vancouver. Peering over the podium, awards judge Stan Persky tells the anxious CALM members that there is some good labour journalism in the award submissions he reviewed, but he calls on the labour movement to start publishing weekly provincial newspapers like the Communist Party's *Pacific Tribune* in British Columbia.

Little did he know that the awards have been affectionately known as the CALMies ever since an incident involving Vancouver's *Fisherman*, a labour paper supported by a largely Communist union readership, and former Canadian Labour Congress president Dennis McDermott, an avowed anti-Communist. When the paper won the top award several years earlier, the red-faced McDermott had to present it in front of the full CLC convention delegation.

Still, Persky was probably right. The Communist weekly and its big sister the Toronto-based *Canadian Tribune* provide some of the best coverage of Canadian labour struggles. But there are earlier models closer to home that Persky might have suggested. Almost any one of the crusading labour newsweeklies that made up the pioneer labour press in Canada could qualify.

I listen as the awards are read out; McDermott is long gone but the *Fisherman* again garners many laurels. As various monthly and quarterly union publications are called, I can't help but notice the glaring absence of a weekly Canadian labour paper, one that could break news stories and publish fresh comments on current issues, a paper that would tell labour's side of the story to a general readership.

Persky breaks into my thoughts with his concluding remarks. "I pay somewhere between $500 and $700 a year in union dues as do at least a quarter of a million other unionists in this province alone," he says. "If . . . someone decided it was important to get our story across on a regular basis, merely using $50 a year of my union dues and those of every other trade unionist in the province would yield a small budget of $12.5 million annually." He drives home the point by sarcastically noting, "I think I might be able to publish a reasonably competitive paper at that price!"

The notion is not so far-fetched. The American labour movement supports the *AFL-CIO News* which still delivers a weekly news package to the nation. West Germany has an alternative daily called *Tag* which gives equal time to labour and business instead of dismissing labour out of hand as the mass media here often do. There is also Britain's *Labour Weekly* which carries soccer scores, television critiques and movie reviews.

A few years ago, *Canadian Labour*, the CLC magazine, published a plea for a "labour-based community press." Journalist Michael Schuller argued that "labour must create its own alternative medium" and proposed "a network of mass-distributed community newspapers based around the district labour council jurisdiction." Schuller calculated that "at a cost of 50 cents per member per month, the labour movement could thus create a newspaper chain stretching from coast to coast with a combined circulation of over four million, making it the largest chain in Canada."

Others have called for a national labour publication to bind the movement together and give it strength to fight the battles for social justice anew. In the early 1970s, a group of the best and brightest in union public relations formed an advisory committee to the CLC. A major project was the founding of a national "journal of labour affairs" tentatively called *Working*.

After much research into costs, frequency, style, even layout design, the group's leaders met with then CLC president Joe Morris to float the idea. Morris dismissed it with a shrug: "What would happen if you carried an ad from a company where an affiliate was on strike?" asked Morris. It was clear the idea would not get his support. Discouraged at this shortsighted attitude, the group soon disbanded.

At a CALM conference in 1987 I jumped into the fray, asking delegates to consider the possibilities of having our own national newspaper. I suggested that we could be leaders in bringing the movement closer together than it's been in years if we had a professionally written and produced weekly that reported in a credible way on labour culture and politics in Canada.

I quoted *Globe and Mail* labour reporter Lorne Slotnick who also saw the value of a labour weekly. "I work on a paper with 25 business reporters and one labour reporter," he said on winning the Wilfred List Award for excellence in labour reporting. "I would like to see a paper with 25 labour reporters and one business reporter." Slotnick encouraged the movement to "start thinking about how they can set up their own news media . . . a labour-financed newspaper or magazine that is independently run but sympathetic to labour."

As Persky completed his judging duties and the winners proudly hoisted their CALM certificates for a photograph, I wondered how many of my colleagues were aware of how significant a role our pioneering ancestors played in building the modern labour movement. Did they share the view that a provincial or national labour weekly, partly modelled on the early labour press, could do much for the modern labour movement by reaching members regularly, preferably through home delivery and even newsstand sales?

Did my colleagues agree that instead of spending millions of dollars annually on mass media advertising, a habit the movement once rejected but now embraces with a passion, the money could be used to set up a national labour newspaper? Would this not be a far more effective way to pull the movement together on major issues?

Would my fellow CALM members conclude, as I had, that labour stands to gain much from promoting and sponsoring an independent weekly labour press for Canada? If such a press were to exist, would not union members be better fortified than ever to achieve the highest goals at the bargaining table? Just as important, would they not finally be well enough informed on issues to perhaps vote for political parties and candidates that defend labour rights instead of those that disregard and even dismantle them?

When the CALM convention ended, I was still left wondering about all these questions. Then a few months later, CLC president Shirley Carr told the annual convention of the Newspaper Guild that "the trade union movement learned long ago that freedom of the press is guaranteed only to those who own one." Perhaps it is time to invest in one, I thought. Then the movement could truly begin to reflect its sizeable constituency back to itself in a credible, human and more meaningful way.

The potential is there for a modern labour press to rouse Canadian workers as never before in their continuing struggle for progressive social change. Some of the inspiration for that struggle is to be found in the pages of the pioneer labour press, and we would be remiss if we failed to learn from it in carrying the movement forward into the 21st century.

Ron Verzuh

"The object of a labour journal should be to report things as they really are, unmask iniquities, uproot prejudices, expose falsehoods, advocate genuine reform, and assist the toiling masses to attain a higher degree of intellectual, moral and social development than they have yet enjoyed."

—A.W. Wright, *Canadian Labour Reformer*, October 16, 1886, Toronto.

"A labour man without a labour paper is like a soldier without ammunition."

—Arthur W. Puttee, *The Voice*, January 4, 1896, Winnipeg.

Introduction

Entrepreneurs of Protest

When R.M. Moore launched the first issue of the *People's Magazine and Workingman's Guardian*, he knew that government officials would be watching him closely. The British immigrant had promised "to uphold the constitution, to defend the impartial administration of justice, support the rights of the people, and make known their grievances." But from the moment the book-sized fortnightly was published in Quebec City on March 16, 1842, its days were numbered.

A copy of what is probably the first attempt at a labour-oriented reform journal quickly found its way into the hands of the provincial secretary for Canada East. Attached to it was a letter from a Quebec City bureaucrat named Robert Russell. He noted that editor Moore was "an idle, drunken fellow [and] merely a tool in the hands of some of our good folks in Quebec."

Who the "good folks" were remains a mystery. They might have been members of the local shipbuilders' union, the seamen's union, or a local painters' union that had formed in the old fortress city high above the mighty Saint Lawrence River. Here their countrymen had fought with Wolfe to defeat Montcalm almost a hundred years before. They were British through and through and would appreciate Moore's reprinting news items from the far corners of the British empire.

By borrowing the name of his eight-page paper from British working-class publications of the 1830s, such as the *Poor Man's Guardian* and the *Workingman's Friend and Political Magazine*, Moore hoped to assure himself some success. By emulating their satirical style, he also ensured the *Guardian* a small but loyal readership. But how long would the authorities allow him to publish what must have seemed to them a treasonous opposition paper?

"The magazine is not intended at present, to be a general political paper," Moore wrote in his first editorial. "Its columns will be confined to the insertion of matters of a local nature, connect[ed] with the best interests of the people." To further placate the cautious Lower Canada establishment he added that "this shall be performed with fearless independence as to persons and parties." Yet it is doubtful that these humble assurances kept Moore out of trouble.

The editor satirized British North American law in articles like "Beauties and Benefits of the British Constitution as Handed Down to Her Present Majesty." He also pressed for reform in the colonies with articles like "Public Men and Public Property: The Quebec Corporation—Unconstitutional Attempt to Tax the People." Among its news items, the *Guardian* also criticized the authorities in articles like "Refusal of Licenses to Tavernkeeps," "Poisoned Imitation Tea," and "The Sheriff of the District of Quebec—His Office and the Duties of It."

It was saucy stuff that could have landed the editor in jail. Such had been the fate of scores of editors and newspaper sellers in his native Britain where the Great Unstamped penny papers circulated free in defiance of the hated stamp tax that required publishers to purchase a stamp for all publications. Like British radical papers of the 1820s, Moore did not embrace the "social question" in any cohesive way, although there was some hint in the *Guardian* of future social concerns such as hours of work, more frequent pay days, and public control of public offices and utilities. If these items didn't push the local powers over the edge, the following call to arms might have.

"The freeborn subjects of the Queen can work a remedy for themselves," Moore urged. "They have the right of petition to his Excellency, the Governor-General; let them act upon that right, and they will hurl to the winds the barbarous attempt of the packed corporate legislators who have dared to deny to workingmen and others, the privilege of an open market, for sustenance of life, from the means they have obtained by the sweat of their brow, on six hard-working days of the seven days of the week."

With this strongly worded broadside, Moore entered into what British media historian Stanley Harrison called the "daring lifestyle of the Radical publisher and editor." He joined the august ranks of countrymen John Wilkes, founder of *The North Briton* (1762), one of the first British reform weeklies, and William

Cobbett, whom Harrison called the "father figure of all the Radicals during a whole long generation." (Cobbett had spent time in Canada as a soldier before buying his discharge in 1791. He then tried to get his officers courtmartialled "for their peculations in the colony," according to Harrison.)

Like these early crusaders for a democratic working-class press in Britain, Moore was "a small enterpreneur of protest living in continual danger." Some of his models were the editors of newspapers that grew out of the powerful British working-class movement known as Chartism. Others came from his adopted homeland—journalistic crusaders like William Lyon Mackenzie and Joseph Howe. Mackenzie had taken on the establishment with his *Colonial Advocate* in the previous decade, leading fellow reformers in the Rebellions of 1837. A few years later Joseph Howe would use the *Novascotian* to attack the government of the day in his home province. His rapier-tongued editorials would bring a charge of seditious libel and lead to one of Canada's most celebrated free speech trials.

In a less flamboyant way, Moore joined them in the push for an opposition press for the colonies even though it is unlikely that the *Guardian* survived beyond a few issues. Not long after his first paper succumbed, Moore resurfaced as the founder of another Quebec City paper called the *Standard*. But it too lasted only a few weeks during November 1842. Nevertheless, Moore had lit the first torch that would eventually fire up a new workers' movement.

The urge to organize trade unions had come much earlier than 1842. For example, dock workers of Saint John, New Brunswick, and Halifax had organized the first unions around the time of the War of 1812. By 1834 carpenters were also organizing into workers' associations and printers had a union by 1837. This suggests that the colonists who settled the new land were not always the happy-go-lucky explorers and coureurs du bois portrayed in Peter C. Newman's books about the fur trade. Nor were they all contented hewers of wood and drawers of water as some historians maintain. Indeed, it is hard to imagine the employees of the Hudson Bay Company or the rival Nor'westers not rebelling over the low wages, horrifying working conditions and repressive managerial style that Newman documents in his colourful trilogy.

Even the earliest navvies, pressed into foreign service by the French explorer Jacques Cartier as he prepared for his historic voyages of discovery in the 1530s, were unlikely to have been passive. Cartier got his crews from French jails full of beggars and poverty-stricken citizens eager to escape such misery, according to Canadian historian Gustavus Myers. But even these wretched beings must have at least contemplated rebellion on occasion, given the harsh conditions of Cartier's voyages and lay-overs in the new colony which he referred to simply as "quelques arpents de neige."

Still, there is no evidence that the land of ice and snow that England and France fought over on the Plains of Abraham in 1763 had trade unions before 1812. Even if there were signs of worker rebellion in the rugged early decades, it could have been put down with brutal and legal force. The British had been well schooled in suppressing dissent, especially through the printed word, since before the first newspapers began appearing in 1622. British immigrants, aware of the jailing of editors and the long campaigns against dissenters at home, might have been understandably reluctant to challenge the authorities by publishing opposition journals such as Moore's.

The fact that printers were among the first workers to establish trade unions would be a boon as the trade union movement began to take shape. The fledgling unions would need to communicate with members and their families. They would need to persuade, cajole and otherwise convince a reluctant labour force of the value of organizing. Printers had the skills to produce newspapers and what better way to educate the immigrant worker?

Such a medium would allow leaders to enlighten the pioneer labourer and artisan with critical views on the social and economic conditions which beset the working classes; immigrant workers could be warned of their fate at the hands of the new country's economic masters. And what a life of misery and destitution they faced!

Unskilled labourers worked six days a week and earned a dollar for each 10-hour day. Skilled craftsman could earn triple that, whereas a woman worker earned only half of a man's wage—perhaps only 35 to 60 cents a day. Children often brought home a pittance of 25 cents. In addition, workers faced high mortality rates, long hours of work, dangerous risks to life and limb, unspeakable living conditions and no social security. There were no paid holidays, no provisions for sickness, workplace injuries or old age. Employers were even known to fire older workers or cut their pay as they exhausted their most productive years.

Nevertheless, it would be several years before another brave soul like Moore stepped into the breach to publish an opposition paper sympathetic to workers and their families. Even if someone had volunteered, the potential for success was limited. Working conditions left workers with little energy to devote to reading of any kind, let alone a labour-political journal that was intent on describing how badly off they were.

There were other reasons why a pioneer labour press was slow to develop after Moore's initial foray. Clearly the new working class did not have much time for reading and study; families were too busy staying alive. But there was also the general problem of illiteracy.

When Canada's first English-language newspaper, the Halifax *Gazette*, began publishing on March 23, 1752, the yet-to-be-constituted nation had less than 25,000 English-speaking inhabitants. Even that estimate may be high, since the bulk of immigration up to 1765 had been from France. Accounts of the earliest British colonists, especially the Irish, show that they were often dirt poor, from socially deprived families, and mostly incapable of reading or writing. Indeed, while journalistic luminaries such as Dr. Samuel Johnson, Benjamin Franklin and Thomas Paine debated freedom of the press, reciting passages from John Milton's *Areopagitica*, the pioneer Canadian working class probably remained largely illiterate.

Things changed as a new century took hold. By 1815, there were about 150,000 English speakers. By 1844, two years after Moore's paper had folded, Upper Canada's population had jumped to 567,000, mostly from Britain. By the early 1870s, when the population of the new country had surged to 2,812,367, there were 1,620,851 inhabitants in Upper Canada where most English speakers had settled. At this point, the problem of illiteracy began to lift, making way for the founding of a labour press.

Still, although Ontario was becoming a highly literate society, the working classes were the last to benefit from the work of early education reformers like Egerton Ryerson. He had worked diligently to create a public school system in the 1840s and 1850s, but it attracted mostly middle-class children whose parents had some property. These children were enrolled in schools that sought to improve the family, the weaknesses of which educators blamed for many social problems. For working-class kids, however, especially those of unskilled labourers, childhood, like adulthood, meant a life of drudgery. Their parents simply could not afford to let them attend school, since mere survival dictated that every family member had to bring home some of the bacon.

As compulsory education was introduced in Ontario in the early 1870s, working-class parents did begin to enroll their children in schools in the hope that education would rescue them from destitution. The future readership of the labour press would be secured, but what of the working-class adult readers that any new paper would have to attract?

In spite of the lack of education and widespread illiteracy up to the 1860s, newspapers did have an influence on the working class. "Much of the supposedly literate population had only an imperfect ability to read," according to media historian Paul Rutherford. This was "obviously an obstacle to the understanding of all but the most simple printed thoughts." However, "there was a fair chance a literate relative or friend would communicate the substance, if not the contents, of a newspaper to the less skilled," he adds. "And not just at home but after church, at work, or perhaps in the tavern."

Illiteracy, then, did not stop the spread of the printed word, nor did it prevent the blossoming of a whole raft of pioneer newspapers. Less than a decade after Moore launched the ill-fated *Guardian*, technological advances in paper making, printing and overseas transportation set the competitive stage for a fledgling media industry. It also raised the possibility of an opposition press growing out of the movement to organize Canadian labour.

Before this, there were no doubt other independent editor-printers like Moore who founded personalized journals sympathetic to workers using outdated machinery for small press runs. But to start and sustain a widely circulated labour newspaper required an established labour movement.

In Britain, for example, where activists had been publishing radical newspapers since 1648, according to Stanley Harrison, the movement was well advanced by the 1820s. Labour papers began to appear "which directly represented the views of the 'journeymen and labourers', and promoted the emergence of the 'general unionism' which was the first ancestor of the modern trade union movement." These papers "began to debate the problems facing the working men as a class—the Political Economy propaganda of the factory masters, the various hopes of escape from this anti-human doctrine, including ideas of Co-operative production and exchange, and the shape of the future, as working men began to feel themselves capable of moulding it." At least 72 such papers had existed by the time Britain legalized unions in the early 1870s.

In the United States, where the movement had a 40-year head start on Canada's, migratory workers found no shortage of labour-oriented newspapers from which to choose. By the early 1830s, there were "not less than sixty-eight such journals upholding the workingmen's cause and agitating for labour reforms," wrote Foster Rhea Dulles in *Labour in America, A History*. "Their enthusiasm and assurance knew no bounds."

John R. Commons in his *History of Labour in the United States* says these papers came out "fearlessly in the advocacy of the principles of the Working Men's Party," and adopted a list of reform measures published at the head of its editorial column by the *Working Man's Advocate* in New York.

Historian Louis Filler says such papers set the tone for future labour struggles for social and economic reforms in the U.S. "With such periodicals as *The Mechanic's Free Press* to speak for it, labour also asked the abolition of debtor's prisons, agitated for free education and free land in the West; it demanded laws which would protect it in the factories and mills," Filler noted.

Between 1863 and 1873, about 120 daily, weekly and monthly labour reform journals appeared, according to Commons. *Fincher's Trade Review*, the first of the national labour papers in the U.S., began publishing on June 6, 1863. Circulated to three Canadian provinces, its support of unionism, co-operation and shorter work hours no doubt influenced the founding of a Canadian movement with its own press.

However, the launching of the Canadian movement was yet to come. Preceding it and perhaps setting the scene for its creation, was the most radical economic and social shift the colonies had ever experienced. This shift brought a new sense of the need for organizations independent of the manufacturing classes to protect workers from the on-coming steam roller called progress.

In 1867, most Canadians earned their living by farming, fishing or logging. These, along with a bit of mining, were the main industries at the time. Basic needs were taken care of by the family farm or through bartering of goods. If someone got hurt or sick, or the bread winner died prematurely, or simply got old, the main support group was the family and neighbours. As the new country industrialized and more people moved to the cities, these informal social security nets weakened.

Rapid industrial expansion in the next decade caused more obvious class distinctions, making the Canadian worker more aware than ever of the changing economic relationship between producer and owner. Many families stricken by the epidemics that swept through Victorian Canada could not afford the available medication. Even if they could have, there was no guarantee that it wouldn't do more harm than good. Old age meant even worse conditions, but still there was no government assistance in the offing. Workers were told to be thrifty, and their children were expected to care for their parents.

The British North America Act, the young country's constitution, invested responsibility for health and welfare in the four provinces, but these were meagre concerns at the time. In the Maritimes, poverty-stricken workers could look forward to the almshouse and the workhouse, holdovers from the Elizabethan Poor Laws of 1601. It was an inhuman way to provide tax-supported aid to the poor, the unemployed and disadvantaged. Upper Canada devised laws which created poorhouses out of jails, and Lower Canada relied on church charity to deal with the social misery that awaited many working-class families.

Any hope of prosperity that the exuberant founding fathers may have persuaded working families to look forward to was quickly dashed by the economic depressions that rocked the new nation in the early 1870s. Renewed waves of depression would hit the young Canadian economy in the mid-1880s and again in the mid-1890s. Unemployment soared, forcing more than one and a half million immigrants to abandon Canada for the U.S. in search of work. Those who stayed eked out a meagre existence and often faced abject poverty. The situation called for government action to provide relief for the poor, but it would be a long time coming. Meanwhile, the prospect of hungry children, shack-like homes and endless hours of drudgery at low pay fuelled the creation of the Canadian labour movement. The hopelessness of 19th-century working life brought militancy to life and gave strength to those who would found the movement. They would take their social crusade to the workers of Canada.

The movement would not be born until four years after the four British colonies had been wedded by Confederation. In 1872, Canadian workers were legally permitted to organize into protective organizations through the passage of Sir John A. Macdonald's Trades Union Act, lifted almost word for word from the British statute books.

Partly in the tradition started by Moore's *Guardian*, the historic struggle for social justice that followed unfolded in the pages of the pioneer labour press. It identified social inequities for working-class readers and proposed various reforms. And its efforts had some impact on the mainstream political parties. Both Tories and Whigs took notice of the new industrial class and began to curry favour with those who founded labour newspapers.

Social reform weeklies, far more radical than Moore's paper ever was, papers such as the *National* and the *Beehive*, also began to appear and successfully appeal to working-class readers. And as both they and the new-found labour press attracted public attention, others saw the pot of gold represented by the working masses. By writing about the plight of workers and criticizing social inadequacies, the labour press pioneers tipped off the daily newspaper barons who proceeded to cater to the workers' desire for news and entertainment.

In the early 1870s, as the working-class movement gathered wind in its sails for the first time, it found its biggest champion in the *Ontario Workman* steered by the able hand of nine-hour advocate James S. Williams. "From then on," literary historian Frank Watt asserts, "a proletarian spirit can be seen evolving in the small radical labour press which struggled to support the interests of that class."

The *Workman* was the first paper with its roots sunk deep in the history of Canadian workers. Its founding spirit flowed from an eclectic blend of earlier movements for social change. It would bring fire and determination to the fight for improved working and living conditions. It would inspire the dedicated men and women needed to breathe life into the new movement, for the Canadian working class was about to enter a period of hardship and struggle the likes of which it had never known.

In a way, the seed for a lasting labour press had been planted by Moore's courageous effort to launch the *Guardian* back in 1842. It had been nurtured by a Montreal labour paper called *Le Peuple Travailleur* which appeared about 1850. Still, before the *Workman* could reach full bloom as the first newspaper endorsed by the labour movement as its chief voice of reform, another entrepreneur, a businessman named Isaac Buchanan and a group of Hamilton railway workers, had to clear yet more trail.

By the mid-1860s, the Hamilton workers, unhappy with the local party press, were set to launch their own weekly. Thought by many to be the first Canadian newspaper published in "The Interests of the Producing Classes," the *Workingman's Journal* primed the movement for the *Workman's* arrival. It is here that the story of Canada's labour press pioneers truly begins.

1

Cradle of a Workers' Press

Isaac Buchanan timed the founding of the *Workingman's Journal* perfectly. As the weekly labour newspaper saw its first printer's ink in the spring of 1864, the Hamilton businessman was making his bid to return to the legislative assembly. He had held a seat for years, supporting the Conservatives in the 1850s and then the Liberals in the 1860s.

If he played his cards right this time, though, the seasoned political war horse could enlist labour's help to handily defeat the mayor of Hamilton in the coming election. It was a key time to be in power, since it was only three years before the four British Crown colonies were to forge a new nation through Confederation. The new government would be instrumental in planning the country's future.

Buchanan wanted to be part of that historical moment and soon his wish would come true. He would be sworn in as president of the council in the cabinet of the coalition government formed by Sir Etienne-Paschal Taché and Sir John A. Macdonald that paved the way for Confederation. But to raise the victory cup, he first needed to collaborate with local Hamilton workers to set up the *Workingman's Journal* to support his campaign.

Buchanan, a Scot who first set foot on Canadian soil at Montreal in 1830 at the age of 19, couldn't have picked a better cradle for the birth of this early worker's journal. The "ambitious little city" of Hamilton was quickly becoming the "Birmingham of Canada." When the first issue appeared on Saturday, April 16, 1864, the city was shedding its image as a potential trading centre. Instead, it was becoming a key manufacturing hub for Upper Canada. Forty-six factories were already in operation, employing about 2,300 workers.

The factory owners and local merchants would surely be willing to pay the eight cents a line for a guarantee that their advertising would reach the local working classes. Buchanan had his finger on that pulse. After all, he was the first president of the Hamilton Board of Trade, and he and his family had built up one of the largest dry goods wholesale businesses in the colonies.

Working families, too, would provide the four-page tabloid with a readership willing to pay the $2-a-year subscription fee. They and other members of the fledgling population of 19,000 could also buy their copies from the newsboys hawking them for a penny in the bustling streets of Steel Town on the shores of Lake Ontario.

Not that they were wooed to the new paper because of Buchanan's staunch advocacy of workers' rights. True, he and his wife Agnes had occasionally contributed to the local mechanic's institute, but Buchanan was not primarily interested in fighting for labour's cause. The new paper offered something quite unique to the working-class population in that it was "Devoted to the Interests of the Producing Classes," as it boasted in its front-page banner. But Buchanan's interest was in using the paper to help him win the election and in espousing his "producer ideology." According to the Buchanan philosophy, workers and factory owners should produce in harmony, thus providing the new nation with all its manufacturing needs.

Buchanan argued for "a reciprocity of interest between small manufacturers and workers," writes historian Greg Kealey, and this "appealed to workers because of its roots in an older society. Moreover, some Tories' emphasis on protection for the encouragement of native industry, their belief in the primacy of labour, their willing acceptance of the labour theory of wealth, their belief in monetary reform, and their empathy and sincere concern for the conditions of workers added to this appeal."

The philosophy might have worked in a community of small businesses and cottage industries, but the thriving city of Hamilton was destined to become a great industrial centre, a stopping off point for the hordes of migratory immigrants looking for factory work in their adopted land. Buchanan's ideology would soon be buried in the rubble as mercantilism made way for the new industrial capitalism of the late 19th century.

Still, Buchanan's ideology had its brief moment in history and the *Journal* provided its voice. His insistent editorial theme stressed the need for a "manufacturer-mechanic alliance." His views on social and economic issues of the day dominated the *Journal's* editorial space. In the June 18, 1864, edition, for example, a review of his book *Industrial Politics in America* took up almost half a page.

The dream of a producers' co-operative commonwealth obviously had some appeal among the workingman's associations and fraternal societies of the day, for the new paper attracted the hearty support of local artisans. In fact, an April 21, 1864, edition of the *Election News* guessed that the paper was "conducted . . . by some of the intelligent mechanics employed in the Great Western Railway workshops, and perhaps other workshops."

It was an impossible dream, of course, since by the early 1870s Hamilton was rapidly shifting to an industrial capitalist economy. Nevertheless, the *Journal* soldiered on. "Everywhere the industrial classes are organizing societies for the protection of their interests and the improvement of their social condition," it crowed in its prospectus. "In the belief that this movement, if carried out on just principles, will do an incalculable amount of good, the columns of the 'Workingman's Journal' will be devoted to its advocacy."

But there would be no cry to foment the revolution in the pages of the Buchanan-backed paper. "The 'Journal' will preach no blind, unreasoning Crusade against the interest of Capital," the prospectus continued, "but will affirm with all the power of reasoning at its command, the right of the producer to an equitable share of that which he produces."

In fact, although Buchanan liked to think of himself as a radical, he hardly fit the mould. If anything, he was an opportunist or at the very best a bundle of political contradictions. As his biographer H.J. Bridgman argues, "he never wanted to destroy the hierarchical structure of society." When William Lyon Mackenzie was blasting the Family Compact during the Rebellions of 1837, Buchanan "rushed to the side of the lieutenant governor whom he had been violently castigating just days before."

Buchanan was not the first to advocate the producer ideology. During the 1850s, "a working man" had edited the *Journal of Industry* in London, Canada West. Its motto was "Self-preservation is the first law of nature." With its focus on "protective tariffs," it also touted the one-big-producing-class idea. Nor was the *Workingman's Journal* the first attempt at a press aimed at the working classes.

Christian socialism, which was based on similar ideals, was a growing movement in Great Britain during the 1850s. The London Working Men's Association had founded the *Christian Socialist*, "A Journal of Association," of which Buchanan was no doubt aware. Over the years, he had become a deeply religious man. As Bridgman has noted, Buchanan viewed his early success in business as God's will. He had become a respected member of St. Andrew's Church while in the Canadas, becoming chairman of its board of trustees, and establishing himself as a pillar of the Scottish Presbyterian community.

The British co-operative movement, also sympathetic to an alliance with the future captains of industry, continued to be a social force long after the successful efforts of wealthy industrialist Robert Owen to found the movement. His *New Harmony Gazette*, published between 1825 and 1835, was still a landmark guide to the precepts of the movement and Buchanan would have been aware of it. Some form of co-operation might have been compatible with his producer ideology, making it a suitable topic for the *Journal*. It was a social ideal that the labour press would embrace off and on throughout its pioneering years.

But Buchanan's business background revealed that he was far from co-operative-minded in his private life. His family's company had long followed a corporate plan that called for strict employee loyalty without offering the workers any say in how the companies operated. The new paper would "elucidate the laws which regulate the remuneration of labour, and discuss the various social questions in which working-men are directly interested." But there would be no room for a sustained debate about the value of co-operation as a solution to the social problems that faced the new industrial classes. Instead, the producer ideology—the marriage of capital and labour—would reign as the supreme social solution in the *Journal*.

In the decades to come, a labour paper which advocated such a cozy partnership would be considered a traitor to labour's socialist cause. After all, the unfettered growth of industry with little or no consideration for the concerns of working people forced the creation of the trade union movement in the first place.

Such contradictions lay beneath the *Journal*'s promise to "consistently enforce the great principle, that the grandeur and power of a nation depends on the happiness, contentment and character of the toiling mass of its people; that their social condition therefore, ought to be the first care of the statesman, the patriot and philanthropist."

Buchanan might have added priest to the list, since the church, including his beloved St. Andrew's congregation, saw most social issues as the sole preserve of the pulpit. An active religious press competed with the *Journal* for working-class readers, and papers like the *Canada Evangelist* and the *Canada Christian Advocate* may have had the upper hand. They often appealed to what social historian Peter Roger Mountjoy has described as the more "conservative" elements of the working class in Victorian Canada.

Despite the suggestion by historian Edward G. Salmon that much of the literature in North American workers' homes was at a "low and vicious level" and that it was "vulgar, sensuous and unwholesome," the religious press, along with early women's journals such as the *Calliopean* and the moralistic Hamilton *Charivari*, continued to proliferate. They pronounced on everything from education reform to the sanctity of marriage and the evils of tobacco. And it was all Buchanan could do to follow their lead in hopes of making the *Journal* "an acceptable family periodical." With 11 little ones on the loose at Clairmont, Buchanan's palatial estate, it was an image he had no difficulty promoting.

The temperance movement, one of Canada's earliest social movements, had as powerful an influence as religion on Buchanan. Temperance advocates likely held their first North American meeting at Sillery, Quebec, in 1648. With the passage of the Dunkin Act in 1854, Buchanan and others promoted the new law's provision allowing municipal councils to prohibit liquor sales if a majority agreed by referendum. By the time the *Journal* came on the scene, there were dozens of temperance publications circulating through Upper Canada homes. Education reformer Egerton Ryerson used his *Christian Guardian* to campaign for the temperance movement and helped spawn one of the first temperance societies at York (soon to be Toronto) in 1830. In 1833, the *Christian Reporter and Temperance*

Advocate became the first New Brunswick movement paper. "Temperance had always exercised some attraction for the craftsman," according to historian Bryan D. Palmer, "and in the 1860s and 1870s the skilled workers who had stood behind the creation of the *Workingman's Journal* and the Hamilton Cooperative Association were undoubtedly temperance advocates."

Another influence on Buchanan's *Journal* was the development of an anti-slavery press in Ontario after 1835, as well as an active immigrant press. The latter had sprung up as British, Scottish and Irish working families began their migration to the New World, particularly after 1815. One of these was Paddy Bennett's *True Liberator*, which began publishing in New Brunswick in 1847 and brought news from abroad to homesick families in the colonies. Bennett proclaimed that he was "concerned about justice, a free press, and the poor man's rights particularly where Irishmen were involved." It was preceded by a much closer historical relative of the *Workingman's Journal* and the later Canadian labour press: R.M. Moore's *People's Magazine and Workingman's Guardian*.

As we have seen, Moore laid the early foundation for a Canadian labour press. Buchanan added an important cornerstone by backing the creation of the *Workingman's Journal* 22 years later, and he clung to some of the mainstays pioneered by Moore, especially news reports from Mother Britain.

Indeed, the *Journal* readership appreciated the news of British workers' organizations and their activities geared to improving social conditions in the homeland. Headlines like "Progress of the Working Man's Club Movement in London," "A Lesson for Working Men" (about co-operatives), and "East London Working Classes," were quick to attract immigrant readers.

Advertisements for British magazines also appeared in the *Journal*, thus appealing to homesick workers and their families. And under headings like "Scraps for the Curious," "Scientific, Useful, Etc.," and "Miscellaneous Gleanings," readers could find tidbits of foreign news. They could also expect to read explanations ("Origins of Boots and Shoes," "The Big Trees of California"), anecdotes, one-liners and maxims. All would become commonplace in labour papers of later decades, as would the *Journal*'s practice of reprinting articles from other newspapers.

While subscribers lapped up the news from abroad, they also insisted on coverage of local labour issues. They got it under headings like "Progress of the Cause" (about new unions forming), "Borrowed Editorials," "Strikes in a Nutshell," and a "Trades Union Directory" (listing union meeting times). Again, all were standard fare in subsequent labour papers.

Despite the obvious usefulness of this variety of editorial fare, the *Journal* did not survive the events leading up to Confederation. Buchanan's dry goods business was in trouble in 1864, and it didn't last out the decade. Five years after the death of his paper, his dream of a worker-owner alliance was still being touted by another editor in the *People's Journal*, which fought for the "protection of home manufactures." But his efforts were in vain. The notion was soon to be bumped aside by a new circle of labour advocates who would have no truck with Buchanan's ideology.

In 1872, the *Journal* founder, near bankruptcy, had to sell Clairmont. It took until 1878 to discharge his debts, while he and his family lived off the charity of friends. The following year, Buchanan received a sinecure from the government on which he lived modestly, but comfortably, until his death in 1883.

In that year, what was arguably the best 19th-century labour paper, the *Palladium of Labour*, would be born. Preceding it, however, and serving as midwife at the birth of the Canadian labour movement and its press, was a group of Toronto printers. They organized Canadian labour's struggle for a nine-hour day, aided in no small measure by the founding of the *Ontario Workman* in the spring of 1872.

2

The Nine-Hour Crusade

James S. Williams didn't waste time stewing in jail after his arrest for seditious conspiracy in the spring of 1872. He and 12 other organizers of the Toronto printers' strike, also arrested for their trade union activities, spent at least some of their time plotting the founding of the *Ontario Workman*, Canada's first true labour newspaper.

As a leader of Local 91 of the Toronto Typographical Union and president of the Toronto Trades Assembly, Williams, along with TTU president and TTA trustee Joseph C. McMillan and fellow master printer David Sleeth Jr., knew the value of reaching union members with a new labour journal. Once Sir John A. Macdonald's Conservatives passed the Trades Union Act later that year, the movement would need information to stimulate organizing drives. It would also need a voice to speak out when Macdonald undermined the act legalizing unions by passing a second clone of Britain's labour statutes, the Criminal Law Amendment Act, which prohibited essential union activities such as picketing and other forms of protest.

As key players in what was becoming known as Toronto's labour junta, the London-born Williams and his Scottish co-conspirator McMillan lobbied hard for changes in these laws. They eventually saw their efforts rewarded when strikes were legalized and official discrimination against workers lessened with the passage of several amendments in the mid-1870s. Through it all, the *Workman* would prove their strongest lobbying tool.

The junta, including future Toronto mayor Edward F. Clarke, knew that they could not count on the daily press to present their views either accurately or sympathetically. They could expect little solace from these papers and might have rotted in jail waiting for the party press to rise to their cause. The *Globe*, owned by the notoriously anti-labour George Brown, could be counted on to blast the printers. During the strike, Brown hired scabs, published fiery anti-labour editorials and made speeches bitterly denouncing the demands for which the printers had struck.

The same new technology, cheap newsprint and improved transportation and communications systems that made it cheaper to produce the new dailies also made it technically easier to start the *Workman*. And the hostile journalistic climate created by Brown made it increasingly desirable for Williams and his colleagues to do so. He hoped his brothers and sisters in the movement would support the idea and that local merchants would be attracted to the paper as an advertising medium ($150 a column inch for a year).

But like any such venture, Canada's first official labour newspaper needed a cause. It found one in the printers' strike and the TTU's demand for a 54-hour work week (nine-hour day) with no decrease in wages. It was a cause that would also serve as what nine-hour movement historian John Battye called the "genesis" of the Canadian labour movement.

The printers' strike ended in mid-March of 1872. A month later, on Thursday, April 18, the *Workman* published its first issue. It was eventually to become the house organ of the TTA, Canada's first city-wide labour central, and the voice of the entire movement. But like other labour papers to follow, the eight-page tabloid hardly riveted the new country's 50,000 industrial labourers to their work benches. At five cents a copy, it was somewhat overpriced compared to the penny dailies. Still, it did appeal to the few thousand activists who wanted news from a labour perspective on the new movement.

Williams declared this lofty ideal under the *Workman*'s logo: "The equalization of all elements of society in the social scale should be the true aim of civilization." He also boasted that the paper would expose "the true cause of all evils that labour complains of," and, "with equal plainness and fearlessness . . . show that a simple and effectual remedy can be applied to the removal of the evils."

The *Workman* began life under the auspices of the Toronto Co-operative Printing Company. But the "outspoken new labour paper," as historians Desmond Morton and Terry Copp describe it, could not survive as a co-op despite the conventional belief in labour circles that co-operation was the best route to social reform for the working classes.

In September 1872, Williams, McMillan and Sleeth, all neighbours on Ontario Street, hatched a plan to rescue the failing paper. Their personal funds depleted, the three men turned to the highest power in the land, Sir John A. Macdonald. The prime minister responded to the call for help by first pressuring cabinet minister Sir Alex Campbell to buy government advertising in the *Workman*. Still, the paper could not sustain itself without much broader support from the movement. However, radicals in the newly built house of labour were reluctant to encourage such support, since they believed that the TTU leaders had curried favour with the Conservatives. The trio's next move sullied their reputation even more.

Believing that the *Workman* was key to the survival of the labour movement, Williams again went to Macdonald. This time he and his cohorts pleaded for a loan so they could buy the paper. The little cabinetmaker, as the prime minister nicknamed himself, promptly sent $500 to the *Workman*. "I don't suppose I will ever get the money," he snorted, "but I may as well keep it over them as security for good behaviour." It was a cardinal sin in the eyes of some labourites.

Bernard Ostry, a student of early Canadian labour and politics, argues that Williams and the others "must always suffer the accusations of having committed an unethical deed by secretly and irresponsibly compromising their supposedly independent labour journal, and thereby jeopardizing the future of their colleagues and of the movement of which they were respected national leaders."

Ostry adds, however, that "as the only recognized working class weekly in trade union hands, it was an invaluable weapon and one can appreciate the owners' desire to keep it running even at the cost of borrowing from its opponents." Critics of the deal felt differently, but in the end it was a tempest in a teapot. Six months after the loan was made, in the spring of 1873, Macdonald had his hands full with the Pacific Scandal. Trying unsuccessfully to hold power under a Grit barrage of charges that he had taken over $300,000 in political donations from the future builders of the national railway, he did not likely have time to worry about the *Workman*. Indeed, "no evidence has yet been brought to light to suggest that Macdonald brought pressure to bear upon the journal to pursue a policy sympathetic to his party," says Ostry, "or that the fact of the loan itself was in any way a barrier to frank and honest discussion of labour problems in the *Workman*'s columns."

With funds secured, the trio agreed that Williams, who had once published the *Uxbridge Times*, would be the paper's new "superintendent." As a first order of business, he promised readers that the paper would "know no party," but would "advocate the repeal of all laws having a class tendency." As the official organ of the nine-hour movement, the *Workman*'s first goal was to cover the fight for shorter working hours with vigorous determination.

The Toronto paper wasn't alone in its support of the movement for shorter hours. Other labour papers sprang up to rally workers around the issue. The *Western Workman* in London, Ontario, "echoed the same themes [as the *Ontario Workman*]," says Steven Langdon in his book on the emergence of the Canadian working-class movement, "attacking the poverty which industrial capitalism brought with it, and stressing the 'inherent indestructive energy' of the working class—'which no power could conquer or overthrow'."

The *Workman's Journal*, probably published in Toronto, may also have been a nine-hours supporter. As was its habit, the *Ontario Workman* advised its readers to watch for this new paper, and it hailed the appearance of the *Journal*, noting that its "columns are unreservedly dedicated to the advocacy of these interests so dear to workingmen, and the ability with which the subjects most closely connected with those interests are handled speaks volumes for its ultimate success."

In Hamilton, James A. Fahey's daily *Standard* had provided sympathetic coverage of the Toronto printers' strike and thus earned the respect of nine-hours leader James Ryan. Fahey's biographer Russell Hann notes that Ryan supported the daily for what he termed its "protective spirit and conservative proclivities." But Williams didn't share the appreciation. He soon condemned the *Standard* for its "mercenary disposition."

"Too long have the labourers of the world been the step-ladders to fame and emolument to designing and unprincipled men," Williams wrote in condemning Fahey, "but in this instance the man in question, though sufficiently mean, had not brains enough to use the working classes at sufficient length to give him competency." Williams predicted that Fahey would cease to be a nine-hours supporter when labour subsidies ceased and the influence of the nine-hour movement that brought them "has ceased to be dreaded by the monied classes."

Having dismissed its only competition, the *Workman* made shorter hours a *cause célèbre* in its pages. Variously called "a social revolution" and "a matter of urgent social necessity," reduced hours of work were seen as a general panacea for many social ills.

Nine-hour advocates reasoned that workers would be able to spend more hours educating themselves, in line with labour's view that education was the great class equalizer. More time to cultivate a healthier, happier family life would in turn mean better social security in old age. Workers would also become more productive because they would be healthier and less tired on the job. "Its supporters claimed that legal limitation of the hours of work would help to relieve unemployment as well as give working men more leisure," notes historian Elizabeth Wallace. For a time some Toronto merchants even supported the idea, thinking it would strengthen their own campaign for earlier shop closings.

In the United States, the shorter hours movement became "a fight for the liberty of the worker," according to historian David Montgomery. Labour radicals saw the movement challenging the very notion of private property. The prominent American labour journal, *Fincher's Trade Review*, stressed the importance of the issue by including the following slogan in its masthead: "Eight Hours, A Legal Day's Work for Freemen."

Despite all the ballyhoo, the movement failed to deliver on the main goal of shortening the work day; that would take a far greater effort and several more years. In fact, although the labour movement put up a radical front through the labour press, it seldom managed to live up to the militant billing it received. It was rarely able to mobilize forces to fight the essentially conservative mainstream political parties.

But, as Battye says, it did bring about the "first newspaper written by and for Canadian workingmen, a vehicle through which working-class aspirations could be expressed without depending upon the doubtful and selective favours of the commercial press." The *Workman* dedicated itself to that chore with great energy. Quickly branching out from the nine-hour issue, the paper argued that "a thorough and general system of education [must be] one of the first duties of the state." And it did "warmly support the principle of UNION among workingmen." The weekly honoured its pledges through commentaries on working and living conditions, critiques of laws aimed at controlling trade union activities, and its coverage of the political dog fights between Grits and Tories vying for the labour vote.

The *Workman* also found plenty of space for dispensing advice, which would become a hallmark of the pioneer labour press. A member of numerous lodges and fraternal associations, including the Orange Order and the Masons, Williams had long cultivated his strong views on proper personal conduct. Few editions passed without at least one lecture on the frivolous purchase of tobacco or alcohol, two of the most readily available escapes from a life of drudgery.

"You are wasting every year in smoke and drink a sum which if saved and taken good care of," Williams wrote, "would make you independent at sixty years of age, or set you up in a business of your own at thirty, with some prospects of success." Workers were told to "fare hard and work hard while you are young, and you will have a chance to rest when you are old."

Williams seldom missed an opportunity to pass on paternalistic preachings. An example: "The highest riches do not consist in a princely income; there is greater wealth than this. It consists of a good constitution, a good heart, stout limbs, a sound mind, and a clear conscience." Similar bits of advice on how to live frugal and clean lives came under titles such as "Starting in the World," "Do the Right Thing," and "Stealing, Lying and Slandering." Such items endeared the paper to temperance advocates and church-goers, but were unlikely to bring about badly needed social changes. Still, Williams filled his paper with some of the liveliest social commentary of the period.

Readers could pick and choose among the many issues of the day. Articles dealt with "Education and Employment for Girls," "A Liberal Land Policy," "Suffrage for Women," "Household Education," "Labour and Knowledge," and "Underpaid Work." The *Workman* offered its subscribers "Foreign," "American," and "Canadian" news mixed with lengthy columns of "Labour Notes" and numerous anecdotes. Moral teachings and tidbits of wisdom and folly were amassed in tiny type under headlines such as "Sawdust and Chips," "Grains of Sand," and "Tales and Sketches."

On the literary page, the paper supplied "a good deal of didactic and hortatory doggerel in favour of the workingman's cause," according to literary historian Frank Watt. "During these early stages of Canadian radicalism the potential power of literature was gradually realized," he suggests, adding that the "seeds of understanding were already present in the *Ontario Workman.*"

Williams did, indeed, publish some bad poetry. But his heart was in the right place. "Despite the editorial view that creative writing was mere entertainment and diversion from the troubles of daily life," he told readers, "we will be invited now and then to turn aside from the turmoil and strife of the world, and find peaceful enjoyment."

Victorian society already sponsored many publications, all of which competed fiercely for the working-class reader's time, money and allegiance. They seldom attempted to represent the nascent labour movement, leaving this domain to the *Workman* alone. But they did appeal to what historian Peter Roger Mountjoy called "working-class conservatism."

In his essay on the politics of the 19th-century British labour press, Mountjoy draws this conclusion: "Whatever the opinions urged from outside, and from a minority of the more educated working classes, it is not unlikely that the predominant working-class attitude was that myopia and resistance to outside influence which leads to real conservatism."

Mountjoy argues that evangelists and political activists could publish until they were blue in the face in an effort to divert working-class readers from their apparently natural course of seeking escapism and pleasure. Such political and religious reading material could only reach workers if they added to the plethora of mass entertainment already available to them from other sources. "All who sought to influence the working classes learnt to copy the techniques of the entertainment press," Mountjoy added, and that included the Canadian labour press founded by British immigrants.

The conservative element was also much catered to by what media historian Paul Rutherford called a "veritable supermarket of newspaper delights" in the late 19th century—various leisure, temperance, religious, family and other entertainment publications. Amidst all the light-hearted humour, popular recipes, and a moral tale or household tip would inevitably come the anti-union, anti-radical bias.

So when Williams opted for the odd poem, serialized a novel or printed a joke, he was no doubt thinking of the *Workman's* survival in a crowded market place. For the paper to carry on, it had to emulate the competition to some extent. To build a readership beyond the labour activists, the *Workman* had to reach out to the more conservative rank and file workers.

This did not mean the paper abandoned its causes. Where it provided "Household Recipes" and the like, it also bolstered the struggle for women's rights. In "Ballot Women," for example, readers were told to "teach them [your daughters] that man occupies no position that woman cannot fill, even to a pair of pants. Teach them that without the ballot woman is simply a cooking and washing machine; that with it she can rule her own little roost. We have plenty of ballot girls, but what we want is ballot women."

Births, deaths and marriages were announced along with often gruesome descriptions of an industrial accident or other tragedies. "On Monday last a man named McGan, employed in the Oakville sawmill, met with a shocking accident, one of his hands being completely severed from the arm," one item reported. "On Saturday last a man named Crosslin, employed in Buck's stave factory, Collingwood, had one of his feet nearly cut off while working a circular saw," another informed readers.

These items indicated the paper's concern for health and safety in the workplace, but they might also have been attempts at some competitive sensationalism. They were interspersed with reports on "Occupations and Health," which listed deaths per thousand in various jobs, and items such as the one that showed that accidents "connected with the liquor business are least healthful," if not "absolutely dangerous."

Politically, the *Workman* had to straddle the line between radicalism and conservatism. Indeed, the *Globe* called the *Workman* "staunch Tory" and "flaming, full-fledged Tory." And historian Bryan Palmer scolded the paper for its failure to "break down . . . the barriers between skilled and unskilled men and women" and its "dependency on paternalistic political figures."

But labour historian Charles Lipton portrayed the aggressive tabloid as "a great model" and "exemplary in its clarity, forthrightness, the way it recorded the workers' struggles and gave expression to their faith." It "led the way in Labour's early efforts for political action" and "practiced the truth that a concern for the people's conditions is a prerequisite of progressive politics and integral culture."

Still, most historians agree that the paper was more interested in social amelioration than in radical social change. "Nine hour leaders [including Williams] clearly believed that only through the pursuit of economic reform in the work place, aided through legislation or co-operation, would economic exploitation be overcome," according to historian Robin Wylie. "There was to be no revolutionary political challenge."

Indignant editorials on labour standards, unemployment and poor wages and working conditions appeared frequently as the *Workman* forged its social advocate image. It noted "the necessity for an improvement in the social condition of our poor," for example, and proposed ways to alleviate unemployment. "It is hoped that the tales of hardship and suffering . . . will go further than merely having public attention directed to them," urged the *Workman*, "and the result be made that strenuous and systematic efforts may be made to mitigate the misery, not so much by doling out with the cold hand of charity, as by inaugurating public works."

Williams also took a strong stand, as did labour editors throughout the rest of the century, against massive government-assisted immigration for the purpose of employing cheap industrial labour even though Canadian workers were available. The issue took an ugly turn when it came to Chinese labourers. As superintendent of the Chinese department at the Metropolitan Sunday School, Williams had a closer relationship than most with the new Canadians. But whatever personal understanding he might have had of the situation was overshadowed by broader labour concerns. Under the heading "The Coolie Traffic," the *Workman* argued that "whenever Chinese labour has appeared it has withered our hopes and blasted what little prosperity life seemed to have in store for us."

Where Williams lashed out mercilessly at one group of workers, he offered his deepest sympathies to another. "There is no greater evil sapping the foundation of our physical greatness as a people than the habit or custom of placing boys in factories and workshops at an immature and tender age," declared an article reprinted from the American *Cooper's Journal*.

Williams warned that the practice of using child labour was "more widely prevalent than many suppose."

Although many families needed the pittance that the children earned, it was clear that society as a whole wanted them out of the workplace and into the classroom. Compulsory education became a reality in Ontario in 1871 and the *Workman* carried the banner high. For Williams, with six daughters, and McMillan, with three sons all destined to be printers, education was a paramount issue and the paper rigorously championed it. In fact, Williams later became a member of the Toronto Public School Board.

"As this grand principle [education] takes deeper root among the masses of our people, Reform shall become more radical and general," Williams wrote. "As one of the Reforms, not in the distant future, that the progressive people of this country shall demand, if we mistake not, is that those to whom is entrusted the lives and liberties of the people shall become more directly responsible to the people."

Literacy historian Harvey J. Graff points out that "to the working class press, the promotion of reading was complex. Reading brought comfort in lonely hours and consolation as well as amusement. To satisfy these needs required varying degrees of ability, some of which would not be held by all literate individuals." The *Workman* therefore "provided instruction in reading skills," and "inveighed against recurring illiteracy and the degradation of education."

Many of the social reforms advocated or lauded by the *Workman* overlapped to some extent. The call for shorter hours that helped launch the paper, for example, raised middle-class eyebrows because it was felt that fewer work hours would mean more hours in the local pub. That, reasoned the Mrs. Grundys of the day, would cause more social problems at home and on the street. Thus the paper generally supported temperance, warning readers to stay away from the 'demon rum' for fear that they and their families would be driven to 'rack and ruin'. The Canada Temperance Act or Scott Act would not become law until 1878, but the *Workman* did its share to ensure eventual passage of the prohibition legislation. The counter-argument was that shorter hours would allow more educational activity such as reading, attendance at public lectures and enrolment in mechanic's institutes. Here's how the *Workman* put it: "An hour a day amounts at the end of the year to 365 hours. In that space how many valuable books may be read, how much pleasure enjoyed in your own home, and how blessed you will be in the gratitude of your own wife and the intimate and cultivated love of your children."

The alcohol problem cut deep into the fabric of society. Temperance historian Brian Harrison demonstrates that governments were not always supportive of workers' efforts to improve their lot through abstinence. After all, this would reduce tax revenues from the sale of liquor. In Britain, for example, the Beer Act of 1830 considerably increased the consumption of alcohol. As well, some labour advocates were critical of the middle-class nature of the temperance movement. Harrison notes that Frederick Engels condemned temperance reformers for failing to see that the workers' environment "made it unrealistic to ascribe their drinking habits to any failure of moral responsibility."

Indeed, as Engels himself had written in 1844, workers were "deprived of all pleasures except sexual indulgence and intoxicating liquors. Every day they have to work until they are physically and mentally exhausted. This forces them to excessive indulgence in the only two pleasures remaining to them." For Engels, and his colleague Karl Marx, the problem called for a more drastic solution than simply restricting the consumption of liquor. But the *Workman* would never fully embrace their proposal for a social revolution to completely overthrow capitalism. Instead, the paper hailed co-operation and other half-measures as the ideal routes to social betterment for workers.

Williams frequently spread the word about one co-op enterprise or another in Britain. He published regular reports on the progress of the co-op movement as the best way to tackle the problems caused by an inequitable system of distributing wealth. Although it was not the revolutionary solution advocated by some, it did offer some immediate hope of respite from a crippling economic system.

John (Cousin Sandy) Fraser explained labour's view of the value of co-ops in an article in his Montreal alternative political paper and *Workman* contemporary, the *Northern Journal*. "It is not simply a question of hours of labour or wages," wrote the former Chartist, "it is a question of social organization, of the true idea of property and what gives a just title to it, of personal estimation and of the relative rank of men; it is a question as to whether a working man shall be looked upon as an economical producing machine; in a word it is social revolution."

The election of Ottawa printer and labour leader Daniel John O'Donoghue to the Ontario legislature in 1874 pushed co-operation into the background. O'Donoghue, called the father of the Canadian labour movement, had proved that a working man could get elected to public office. Williams saw the potential and, although stopping short of a call for universal suffrage, he advocated the vote for workingmen without property. Since only property owners could vote at the time, many workers were without the franchise. These new votes could help more labour candidates get elected and help bring "a more just and equitable distribution of the comforts, aye, even the elegancies of life," Williams argued. "The rich getting richer, the poor growing poorer, is now the social order," he wrote, "and as the poor grow poorer so does their servility to the rich increase."

The *Workingman's Advocate* in Chicago put it differently in an article Williams reprinted. "The tendencies of capital to centralize; of railroads to monopolize; of corporations to combine; and of legislation to discriminate in favour of interests proportionate to the wealth they represent, are omens of evil, and the harbingers of oppression, fatal to the life, growth, and development [sic] of the dearest interests of the labouring classes."

Support for labour candidates became a preoccupation for Williams and company. Beyond debunking the myths propagated by the two mainline political parties or supporting the labour candidates who sought to defeat them, it was also a matter of battling the daily press. The *Workman* recognized the social value of the popular press. "The newspaper is just as necessary to fit a man for his true position in life as food or raiment," cajoled one editorial. "Show us a ragged, barefoot boy, rather than an ignorant one. His head will cover his feet in after life if he is well supplied with newspapers. . . . Give the children newspapers." But Williams saw red whenever it came to political issues and the dailies.

Every effort "to secure to labour it[s] just reward is howled down by the 'press'," the *Workman* complained in an early mudslinging match with the dailies. "A corrupt newspaper, like the deadly Upas tree, poisons all who come in contact

THE NINE-HOUR CRUSADE / 31

with it." Ironically, the *Workman* and papers that followed slammed the commercial press, while borrowing from the peoples' journals which were publishing some of the best social affairs reporting of the time. Even its readers got into the act. "Accustomed as I am to see questions of the first importance perverted and distorted, their advocates misrepresented and maligned," wrote one reader, "yet I must confess the *Globe* out-Herods Herod in its mode of discussing anything relating to the labour movement in this country." Other readers took pot shots on a letters page which became as popular for Canadian working-class readers as Hyde Park on Sunday for the British.

In order to bring the Canadian worker such a variety of weekly news, entertainment and commentary, the *Workman* struggled to pay its own way through subscriptions and advertising. (There were ads for everything from fine handmade cigars to sure-fire cures for cancer and the latest in men's and women's apparel.) But it seems that the bulk of the work force in the early 1870s was not prepared to support an independent labour press.

With the help of the prime minister's loan, the *Workman* stayed alive for about two more years, giving it a longer life than many of the labour papers that followed it. But by 1874, the paper was forced to suspend publication. Williams had again run out of cash.

As Lipton explains, this time a more appropriate saviour came forward in the form of the Canadian Labour Union, the country's first national labour central. Delegates to its 1875 convention, including McMillan representing the TTU, realized what a loss the collapse of the *Workman* would be and offered to bail out the weekly. The convention proceedings read: "Believing that the education of the working men of the Dominion in matters affecting relations between labour and capital is the surest way of awakening their interest and co-operation in the cause of union and labour reform, and believing that the establishment of a labour newspaper is the best means of obtaining that object, The Canadian Labour Union pledges itself to use every legitimate means in its power to support any newspaper that may be established to reflect the views of the masses of our working men in matters affecting their welfare."

The CLU boost helped Williams struggle on until early 1875 when the paper closed its doors for a second and probably final time. There is some evidence of an attempt to revive the paper as late as 1877, by which time McMillan had become treasurer of the CLU and a member of its parliamentary committee. But the *Workman*'s demise was clearly at hand and the young labour movement would be left without a strong social advocacy voice during a period of deepening economic depression and social malaise.

Some of the legislation that labour had been calling for had passed by 1877, but the movement was too weak to do anything about the failure of both the Liberals and the Conservatives to bring about the meaningful social legislation needed to improve the conditions under which working families lived and worked.

As the decade came to a close, Williams and McMillan carried on building the new movement and continued to run their printing firm. Williams, who had learned the printing trade in a Methodist book room, stayed in the commercial printing business until his retirement. By 1881, the two friends were busy founding a new central labour body which would become the powerful Toronto Trades and Labour Council. From 1882-84, McMillan ran a book store which was a centre for labour activity and acted as an agent for the *Trades Union Advocate*, an organ of the rapidly expanding Knights of Labour. The new organization was a marked departure from the old concept of craft unionism pioneered by the Toronto junta. It would demand the unionization of all workers and a more sweeping brand of social change than was ever conceived in the *Workman*.

But the fact that there were no major social advances during the period when the junta was in control of the movement does not mean that the *Workman* failed in its mission. The paper was in many ways conservative, but it was a step ahead of the Tory producer ideology that Isaac Buchanan had so earnestly embraced in the *Workingman's Journal* a decade earlier.

In fact, the Toronto paper had revealed the first real signs of a working-class consciousness—what Watt calls "a proletarian spirit . . . in the small radical labour press which struggled to support the interests of that class." This spirit "manifested itself in disillusion with and radical criticism of the programme of nation-building," he wrote, and "in an inclination to associate the patriotic forces which supported the National Policy with the motives and methods of capitalist exploitation."

Whether this radical spirit grew out of the working class itself remains undocumented. Long hours of hard labour may have kept most workers from developing the same keen consciousness of social ills as the labour press expressed. Still, many of the issues debated and highlighted in the *Workman* during the nine-hour movement's heyday resurfaced again and again in the years to come.

As the capitalist economy became more sophisticated, workers and their families became increasingly aware of the injustice of their situation. Their best source of information for becoming aware was the labour press. It was there and through the rise of trade unions that they began to understand the nature of their oppression, of class divisions in Victorian society, and of the importance of uniting to change it.

3

A Maritime Miners' Friend

When a worker for the Spring Hill Mining Company pushed a parcel of scribbled note paper towards Robert Drummond, the former Halifax journalist didn't hesitate. The editor of the *Trades Journal*, Canada's first Maritime labour weekly, was nearing his deadline and he needed something spicy for the 2,000 readers who dutifully paid their three cents for the Wednesday tabloid.

Almost 40, Drummond had started the paper on January 8, 1880, displaying a firm resolve to live up to the slogan "Devoted to the Interests of the Mine, the Workshop and the Farm." The worker's article, a political skit, was certain to fit the bill, Drummond thought. After all, it took a poke at the same mining company in which he was once employed "as a Scotsman low in the management hierarchy [an overground supervisor]."

Once, while writing under the byline Traveller for a Halifax daily which supported the Liberal Party, Drummond had also taken some pot shots at the company. He had been fired for his efforts, according to historian Sharon M. Reilly. Now that he was working for the Provincial Miner's Association, the union that was picking up the bills for the new labour journal, he wasn't going to let the same fate befall the PMA member who had submitted the political skit.

When the four-page newspaper appeared with the worker's item in it, a local mining company official came after Drummond with a vengeance. He wanted to know the author's name. The *Trades Journal* editor refused. The next thing Drummond knew, he had the first of two libel suits slapped against him and his irreverent sheet. (The second came after Drummond published a statement about gas in the mine supplied to him by the deputy inspector of mines. The editor recalls in his memoirs that the "case was laughed out of court.")

The style of this Maritime labour advocate was described by his successor John Moffat as "aggressive, energetic and fearless, yet . . . moderate." Through the *Trades Journal* he would add his mark to the rich east-coast tradition of radical journalism. Over 50 years before, a patriotic Haligonian named Joseph Howe had blazed his way into the history books with the *Novascotian*, a weekly thorn in the side of Tory officialdom. Howe saw the local Tories as the chief enemy of freedom of the press in the British colony and he set out to do something about it. As noted earlier, the powerful blows he struck for press freedom landed him at the centre of the most celebrated criminal libel trial in Canadian history. They also helped him to attain the high office of premier.

Hugh Finlay, president of Local 85 of the International Typographical Union in Saint John, New Brunswick, had also made a notable contribution. He had been publishing a sheet called the *Printer's Miscellany* since 1876. The ITU activist called his paper an "exponent of printing and all the kindred arts," but within that mandate he included labour issues.

In the tradition of Howe and Finlay, Drummond took his place in the annals of Maritime journalistic history. By the time the PMA began in 1879, the Maritimes had developed distinct socio-economic patterns directly tied to the 200-year history of the region's coal industry. This called for an equally distinct trade union movement and Drummond was to be a key player in shaping it. Although he didn't become premier, he too eventually entered provincial politics as a Liberal. It seemed a natural progression, since his all-consuming passion was politics.

A "cautious and genial Scotsman," as historian Eugene Forsey has called him, Drummond drafted the constitution of the Provincial Workmen's Association—the name had been changed in the early 1880s to reflect the view published in the *Trades Journal* that "Every miner is a workingman, but every workingman is not a miner"—and would be the organization's grand secretary for 19 of its 38 years.

In his draft constitution, he forged the editorial path the *Trades Journal* was to take. The first object of the new miner's society was "to advance materially its members, by promoting such improvement in the mode of remuneration of labour as the state of trade shall warrant or allow, and generally to improve the condition of workingmen morally, mentally, socially, and physically." But Drummond quickly qualified that goal with another statement: "Our object is not to wage a war of labour against capital . . . on the contrary, by mutual concessions between master and man, we seek to have it [trade] carried on with advantage to both."

The tone was reminiscent of the philosophy espoused by Isaac Buchanan's *Workingman's Journal* almost 20 years earlier. But Spring Hill (later renamed Stellarton) was far removed from the industrial heartland, and the economy in Nova Scotia was not about to convert to industrial capitalism as it was doing in central Canada. If the notion of a worker-employer alliance were to be to the advantage of working people, it might last here longer than elsewhere. Also, as Drummond notes in his memoirs, the PWA had a stronger influence in the legislature than did other labour bodies. "Any influence exerted by the *Journal* was due to the fact that it was the mouthpiece of the PWA, with a membership large enough to secure the attention of the legislature," he happily admitted. "In fact, on looking over the list of benefits I am not sure but the *Journal* carries off the palm for the largest number of reforms."

By early 1882, Drummond had changed the paper's slogan to read "Unity, Equity, Progress. None Cease to Rise but Those who Cease to Climb." It was meant to signify a broadening of the paper's editorial scope. He was also boasting that the paper would soon have 2,000 subscribers. In his memoirs, Drummond lists some of the issues the paper raised as chief concerns of the PWA. A main item was better education in the form of mining schools and night schools for boys working in the mines "at the early age of twelve—and sometimes at an earlier age." Better wages and more frequent pay periods were also crucial, the latter to keep workers from falling into deeper monthly debt. Better home life through shorter hours of work and improved housing were also priorities. So were government-assisted relief societies, "which did incalculable good, and which a majority of miners voted was preferable to the Compensation Act."

What the memoirs don't indicate is that the *Trades Journal* editor was largely responsible for bringing those social issues to the fore. Labour historian Harold Logan has commented that the "ready pen of the able and educated grand secretary was an important force in laying the foundations and colouring

the thought of the organization, in airing the miners' grievances, and in establishing a recognition for the Association
beyond its immediate membership."

The paper gained its most loyal readership under Drummond's carefully preserved pseudonym, Rambler, and it was
his column "Rubs by a Rambler" that helped the weekly measure up as a sometimes sassy labour paper that seldom forgot
the social interests of the working classes in the Maritimes.
The pen-name was reminiscent of his earlier efforts at ano-
nymity when he was signing his freelance articles "Traveller."
Bylines like these were designed to give readers a sense of
adventure and mystery, inducing them to read about the exploits
of their intrepid correspondent. Drummond usually delivered,
especially when it came to popular social causes.

The editor took great pleasure in using the Rubs column
as a battering ram against what he perceived as the social evils
of the day. Like other labour editors before him, he supported
temperance as an all-around solution and attacked the "rum-
sellers" and all those who opposed the movement. Not even
such an august body as the Canadian Senate escaped the sharp
quill of the Rambler. "Temperance legislation made no progress this year owing to the attitude of the Senate," he wrote in
one spirited column. "No; and as long as the Senate is allowed
to do just as they please, temperance or any other legislation,
that has for its object the social and moral welfare of the people, will never make any progress."

Get rid of liquor—"labour's curse"—and all other social
problems will wane, the *Trades Journal* counselled, and it did
its fair share of rabble-rousing for the cause. In one report on a
juvenile temperance meeting, for example, the weekly noted
that "ten or a dozen young lads . . . acknowledged . . . having
broken their pledge [to swear off liquor]. The question may be
asked, is parental authority exercised, or is parental affection
dead?"

Like the *Ontario Workman*, the *Trades Journal* usually sided
with social reform rather than revolution as the preferred strategy for achieving change. Since temperance was acceptable to
all classes, it was much easier to advocate than some less
popular, more radical movements for social improvements.

Trade unionism was, of course, the most important movement. "We confess that we are amazed at the hostility shown
by some managers towards their workmen on account of their

being in connection with what is popularly called a Union," Drummond wrote. He urged readers to unionize and to pattern the union on political activities engaged in by an organization similar to the PWA which had started at the same time in his native Scotland.

The editor also called on the government to grant the vote to all workers. "Let every resident be registered as a voter," he proposed, "and let him vote only in the district in which he is registered, whether or not he has property in any other district." The *Trades Journal* rallied around the creation of sickness and benefit societies, but railed against Louis Riel, the Metis leader who was causing a furore in Ottawa with his Prairie land claims rebellion. He "ought to have been hanged long ago," Drummond opined.

Rambler's moralistic tone, reminiscent of some of Williams's writings in the *Ontario Workman*, carried over into the rest of the paper. "The fact that wealth is not evenly distributed, should not . . . cause workingmen to fold their hands and mourn over their inequality," he wrote in one of those hard-work and save-for-a-rainy-day items so common in the pioneer labour press, "but should rather stir them to renewed exertion."

The high moralism did not exclude social affairs reporting and commentary. Drummond filled the columns with views on all the key issues, with health care and occupational safety being paramount. The well-educated editor even ran a "Health" column on the front page, indicating that the issue was high on the paper's list of social priorities.

The occurrence of mine explosions or cave-ins struck fear into the hearts of workers and their families. In the event of such a mishap, they stood to lose loved ones and often faced a lengthy stay in the poorhouse. Drummond, who had once worked at the coal face in Cape Breton's Lingan mine, knew the frustrations caused by unsafe working conditions and he used the *Trades Journal* to speak out on the subject. The lack of sick benefits, poor safety standards and too few safety inspectors were regular editorial topics. So was the need for a workers' compensation act.

In an editorial on the British compensation system, which allowed workers to sue for damages, the *Trades Journal* suggested that "it might be well that in Nova Scotia a workman could sue the managers for damages when he receives an injury to which he has in no way contributed. It might quicken inspection, and make some more vigilant."

Mental health and asylums were also of interest, although they were often treated more as a source of humour than as signs of serious social disorder. One item even called attention to "A Lunatic's Newspaper." The writer observed that "As a rule, the articles display marked ability, and no one would suppose that the writers were suffering from mental aberration."

Poverty and old age security took their place near the top of the list of concerns. In one Rubs column, for example, Drummond backed a bill to abolish imprisonment for debt. He argued that it "will have a tendency to put a check on the credit system which is more a curse than a blessing, expecially to the workingmen." In an item titled "A Child's Rebuke," the writer laments the lack of a social security system to care for the elderly. "An old man whom age had made helpless and decrepit was obliged to depend entirely for his subsistence and care upon his son's family."

Housing, too, was a major social concern. A story headed "Land Policy" noted that "Many of the workmen of the Halifax Company would gladly build houses of their own, did the Company have sufficient sense to encourage them in doing so, by offering lots of land at moderate prices." It was not company-built housing that Drummond advocated, but a fair chance for workers to build their own homes and therefore gain the right to vote.

To some extent Drummond saw education in a similar light to Williams at the *Ontario Workman*. It was a source of salvation and a long-term answer to many social problems. But the *Trades Journal* focused more on improved education for miners so that they might know more about the scientific basis of their trade than on promoting compulsory education. It emphasized the need for night schools so that miners' sons could work during the day and bring home badly needed wages.

Drummond noted with pride that of 500 boys in the Nova Scotia collieries, not more than 12 could not read and write compared with the exact opposite situation in Montreal factories. But then he also argued that "Not only is excessive brain effort in youth no help toward developing intellectual greatness in manhood, but it is an actual hindrance." In a rare mention of schooling for girls, Drummond reprinted an item which noted that an eight-year-old girl "died of brain fever brought on by over study."

Drummond fought hard on behalf of both boys and girls when it came to the "barbarous" practice of sending children to work at "so early an age." The *Trades Journal* abhorred child labour in its editorials, yet somehow the editor did not see fit to extend his sympathy to another badly exploited group in society—the Chinese immigrant worker.

Like the *Ontario Workman* before it and most later pioneer labour papers, the *Trades Journal* was openly hostile towards Chinese labour, even publishing racist slurs in its campaign against the federal immigration policy. Quite simply, stated the weekly, "We have no room for them in Nova Scotia." Drummond and others justified their attitude by claiming that Chinese immigration caused undue job competition. But this was hardly an adequate excuse for the outpouring of slights on the living habits and customs of "that heathen Chinee." It was a black mark on the paper's otherwise fine record as a social advocate.

Women earned somewhat more sympathy than the Chinese, but it isn't easy to assess how progressive the *Trades Journal* was on issues concerning women. On the one hand, Drummond supported women workers on strike. One item noted that "Some five hundred girls employed in the cotton mills of Gould, Pearce & Co., struck for a reduction of a half hour daily off the time of work." On the other hand, there was always room for a comment on the biological and intellectual inferiority of the 'fairer sex.' "It has long been proved, to woman's satisfaction, at least, that she is mentally man's equal, and with this knowledge, in many cases, has come the desire to prove the equality by persistently pushing herself into his functions," wrote one irate contributor. "Such persistency goes a great way, in my mind towards proving her ignorance and inferiority."

Inflammatory arguments like that one may have helped to keep readers coming back. But Drummond knew he was always in competition with the commercial press to retain the interest of PWA members. Thus the bizarre and often unsavoury side of life—the inexplicable and the unbelievable—found almost as much space in the *Trades Journal* as the local and provincial news.

No one could claim the former journalist didn't have an eye for the human interest story. He knew exactly which yarns would have the most widespread appeal among his readers. Instead of local news on the front page, he gave them graphic depictions of news from afar. "A coloured man murders his children," noted one headline. Another spoke of the "terrible condition of the Russian peasantry." On the domestic scene, "Hints for the Household," the "Mines Report," and "Farmer's Corner" also found their place in the paper, alongside a generous offering of poetry, fiction, anecdotes, advice and the "final utterances of distinguished people on their death-beds."

On political questions, it was not Drummond's style to advocate truly radical solutions to social problems. One writer, for example, extolled the values of co-operation as the "sole path by which the labouring classes as a whole, or even in any large number, can emerge from their condition of hand to mouth living, to share in the gains, and honours of advancing civilization." In fact, Drummond regularly lectured his readers on the "curses" of "socialism and communism."

As we shall see, he had political aspirations beyond the labour movement which would not be well served by radical posturing in the *Trades Journal*. The closest he came was to quote others on such solutions. One left-leaning writer who met with Drummond's approval was Dr. J.G. Holland. In his series, entitled "The Capitalist and the Labourer," he often sharply rebuked the system. "To corporations, a workman is a machine, running by vital power, to be supported at the lowest cost, that he may help pay a dividend," he wrote. Another writer concluded that "As surely as the nineteenth century is drawing to a close, so surely the march of events is bringing the civilized world to a social revolution."

For Drummond this was a frightening prospect. Unlike later pioneer labour editors, he believed it had to be discouraged as a most fatal course for the working classes. In his view, "The stone deaf ear turned to the cries of labour, by statesmen, by reformers, and by the clergy, is chargeable with much of the wild communistic spirit, that has seized on many in the lower ranks of life." The editor was bound to steer a more moderate course in his newspaper and in his own political career.

The *Trades Journal* provided an unfettered outlet for all of Drummond's views and he used it as a political vehicle for achieving the PWA's political goals . . . as well as his own. Early in the *Trades Journal*'s life, he proudly told readers that workers would play a "leading part in politics in the future and take a more determined stand than in the past." Under Drummond's guidance, the PWA became a strong lobby for legislative change. It pushed for reform of mining laws, called for an effective lien act so workers would be sure to receive payment for their labours, and supported the creation of an arbitration board.

When W.S. Fielding and his Liberals took power in the 1882 provincial election, Drummond gave his tentative approval. The new government would not be opposed by the *Trades Journal*, so long as it did not "show any inclination to treat workingmen . . . with indifference, if not disrespect."

Support for the Grits did not come lightly to Drummond. He had been a staunch Conservative and was only persuaded to shift his allegiance by the view that the Tories were too close to the mine managers. In the debate over an arbitration bill which finally became law in 1889, much to the *Trades Journal*'s credit, Drummond explained his switch. "With a Liberal government in power, who owe nothing to the managers," he wrote, "arbitrators will not be selected who have leanings toward capital. With a Conservative government it might be different. The managers are their mainstay in the mining counties."

In 1886, Drummond fully declared his Liberal support by running as an independent Liberal candidate in Pictou County. His decision to do so was "cause for much consternation and scandal," according to historian Joe MacDonald. In its belief that Drummond had been co-opted by the Liberals, the labour vote was split between two labour candidates. The result was the election of a Liberal, unseating the Tories after 19 years of rule in the county. Drummond was incensed. The workers "have not been able to throw off the shackles of party," he wrote, and he blamed their "apathy and indifference, if not open hostility," for his defeat.

The editor justified his move to the Liberals repeatedly in the *Trades Journal*. "Any system of representative government that does not include not only the representation of the great wage-earning class, but their representation on the floor of the Dominion or Local house by some of themselves is a mere farce," he protested in one article. "Conservative as I am in my leanings," he wrote in his Rubs column, "I cannot approve of any system that is likely to interfere with the obtaining [of] the true voice of the people in the matter of representation." But the opprobrium that came with his switch to the Liberals would not disappear.

Regular coverage of political developments in "Parliamentary Summary," "Local Legislature," and "Dominion Parliament" attests to the paper's efforts to raise working-class awareness of the importance of labour representation in government. Under the heading "Workingmen and Politics," the editor encouraged miners to form workingmen's political clubs. "They need not expect to receive their rights, to have even scant justice done them far less any favours granted, until they have clearly demonstrated at an election, that they are a power, and that separate and apart from the managers."

In 1889, Drummond won election as a town councillor for Stellarton. But this also tainted his image as an independent labour candidate, since he had been nominated by a coal manager. Later that year, he further damaged his political career by failing to respond negatively to the calling out of the militia to end a strike at Lingan mine.

Part of his political misfortune was due to the anti-labour and anti-Drummond bias of the established press. The editor openly blamed the media for much of the political difficulties of the labour movement. Indeed, the Rambler scorned the "slavish" party press. In one editorial comment, he wrote that "the people are kept divided and arrayed against one another by political bosses, while they are poisoned by a venal and subsidized press."

In his memoirs, Drummond says the majority of dailies opposed his views: "Some of them—the minority however—were not only bitter but venomous in their opposition." Their editorials denounced the claims of workers voiced in the *Trades Journal* as "dangerously communistic," and they acted as an "enemy to unions." Drummond confesses that this made for much "thrusting and parrying" and a "lively, and yet, on the whole, an enjoyably exciting time."

Of course, the press did not take the criticism lying down. The *Sydney Express* slammed Drummond as having "a career of idleness" and of using the *Trades Journal* to vent his "personal hostility" toward mine owners. The *Sydney Herald* charged that the *Trades Journal* was hypocritical in first advocating protection against coal duties, then softening its editorial stance.

The *Antigonish Casket* and the *Cape Breton Advocate*, both stalwart Catholic Tory papers, went after Drummond's hide on religious grounds. The *Casket* charged that the *Trades Journal* had engaged in "anti-Jesuit agitation" by publishing an anti-Jesuit writer, "who in Pictou County attacked the Catholic Church in general and one of its priests in particular." The *Advocate* complained that Drummond had written "a liturgical form of some kind, to be used as a service in the burial of dead [PWA] members." The paper said this was a flagrant attempt to come between Catholic miners and their church.

With the creation of the Maritime Press Association in 1888, the feud between the labour and commercial press lost some of its bite. J.J. Stewart of the *Halifax Herald* was among the 24 newspaper representatives at the founding convention. He and James McQuinn of the *Halifax Chronicle* sat in the same room with Drummond and talked of establishing an association of newspaper reporters not unlike the PWA which they had heavily criticized for years.

Drummond was made vice-president of the association and was asked to draft its constitution. The association was created to serve as a union in that its principal aim was to better "conserve their [newspaper reporters'] rights, secure legitimate privileges, and, generally to protect, preserve, and promote their interests," as he noted in the *Trades Journal*.

In 1891, Premier Fielding rewarded Drummond for his loyalty by appointing him to the province's legislative council, a body similar to a provincial Senate. Ironically, Drummond had advocated abolishing it only a few years before. That year also marked a major change in the *Journal*. After 11 years as the east coast's principal social advocate, and probably the longest continuously published labour paper in the 19th century, Drummond officially declared it quits. From his council appointment until he retired in 1924, he would advise the government on the coal industry.

He had bought the PWA's interest in the paper back in 1884 by paying $500 for the printing press. From then on the PWA had paid him a biannual stipend of $500 to run the paper in the best interest of its members. Drummond had done that. Now it was time to return to his early roots as a journalist. He converted the *Trades Journal* into a community weekly called the *Journal and Pictou News*. The new paper continued to publish until 1898, but its role as a labour advocate diminished greatly. In its opening editorial, Drummond, then 51 years old, promised not to "bore our readers with long so-called editorials, nor will we go to the other extreme by catering to what we believe a depraved taste for small gossip and scandal." He concluded that "we may confidentially inform those who are afraid to blow their noses, lest it be publicly noticed, that they can blow till they are blue so long as they do not burst a blood vessel."

Drummond carried on as grand secretary of the PWA until 1898, when he resigned to found the *Maritime Mining Record*, which survived until a year after his death in 1925. With the demise of the *Trades Journal* and the end of the Drummond era, the PWA embraced a new labour newspaper called the *Searchlight*. Edited by C.W. Lunn, who likened himself to Joseph Howe, the PWA leadership was attracted to the paper's "non-political" or non-partisan approach and its support of temperance, according to historian Ian McKay. Although it isn't certain how long it remained the PWA organ, the *Searchlight* continued to publish until 1902.

The United Mine Workers of America, founded in 1890, would eventually move into the mines of Nova Scotia. But before that, the PWA would come under steady attack from the powerful Knights of Labour. The massive United States-based union raided PWA lodges in the late 1890s, almost destroying the old Maritime miners' union.

As Drummond was building the PWA and his *Trades Journal* in the east, the Knights were making their mark on the labour movement elsewhere. By the early 1880s, Hamilton, Toronto and Montreal had become centres for Knights organizing activities. Thousands of workers, especially in the industrial heartland of Ontario, had been excited by the idea of one big organization of workers based on whole industries rather than the narrow craft structure which limited membership to specific trades.

The Knights saw the strength that would grow out of a movement built on the democratic principle of all for one and one for all. Organizing whole plants of workers, rather than exclusive classes of workers who had a trade, would create an unbeatable multitude of unionists. Helping to drive home the Knights' message and inspire workers to join this multitude was a new kind of labour press, one that would reject the mild-mannered approaches to social criticism that had marked the *Trades Journal*.

4

Agitate, Educate, Organize

Toronto printer Eugene Donavon didn't care much for party politics. He'd watched the two mainline parties make their hollow promises through the 1870s, as the new country struggled to its feet. He knew the importance of placing labour sympathizers in the legislatures, but he viewed most Grit and Tory politicians as "creatures of circumstance, who regulate their actions by expediency."

Seven years after the Noble and Holy Order of the Knights of Labour first secretly set foot in Canada, establishing Local Assembly 119 at Hamilton in 1875, Donavon was on the eve of launching a new labour journal for Toronto workers called the *Trades Union Advocate*, the first Knights paper in Canada. Its slogan was "Non-sectarian— Non-political," and the prominent member of the Toronto Typographical Union fully intended to "steer clear of political quicksands."

The new paper could not "properly fill its mission," he wrote in the first edition on Thursday, May 4, 1882, "if it panders to politicians." Donavon knew of only one other labour journal publishing at the time—Bob Drummond's *Trades Journal* out on the east coast—so the aim of his three-cent tabloid was no less than "the advancement of all legitimate labour interests" for workers throughout the young dominion. It was a hefty challenge, and one that Donavon felt could not be left solely in the hands of the law-makers. Instead, he pledged his first allegiance to independent candidates schooled in the Knights credo of "Agitate, Educate and Organize."

The order had been founded as a secret society at Philadelphia in 1869 and its leaders had watched in awe as the new movement charted its meteoric rise in popularity. Soon it captured the imaginations of more than 12,000 workers in more than 400 Knights assemblies north of the 49th parallel. The

Knights' arrival on the Canadian scene greatly radicalized the labour movement's perspective on social issues.

For some it was a new religion to be embraced with evangelical enthusiasm. Others saw in it many of the qualities of friendly societies, with its bizarre rituals and associational style. Still others related to the Knights as a political reform movement that could add great strength to the still growing labour movement.

Such diverse and widespread appeal vastly enlarged the constituency of the movement and helped forge an energetic labour press to carry the word to the burgeoning Knights membership. Donavon was at the forefront of it all. Deeply committed to unionism and the social vision of the order, he believed that labour representatives in the legislatures—candidates trained in the Knights philosophy—were the best hope for the workers. Although he would eventually renounce his support for politicians of any stripe, at first he saw the election of such candidates as necessary for social advances.

The *Advocate* embraced the labour or industrial unionism espoused by the order. It provided its readers with plenty of news on how and where the Knights were organizing. Women were given more prominence with the coming of the new style of unionism; they were treated less as an anomaly and more as workers with an equal need for union support. Shorter hours of work and temperance, while still important, were joined by more all-encompassing solutions to labour's social concerns.

Social palliatives proposed by the great social theorists of the day were the source of much editorial debate. Henry George's *Progress and Poverty* argued that land monopoly was the root of all inequality. He outlined schemes for land nationalization and a single tax which would tax wealthy landowners, appropriating the rent they extracted for the use of their land and using it to pay for social improvements. Edward Bellamy's classic novel *Looking Backward* also carried great influence among labour advocates of the period with its frightening vision of what the world was becoming under capitalism. The *Advocate* distilled the new theories for its readers, bringing them hope at a time when a depressed economy had kept the working classes in penury through much of the 1870s, and was soon to bottom out again with full force in the mid-1880s.

Donavon recognized the appalling injustice of the working and living conditions that Canadian families faced. Like many, he was shocked and angered by the findings of the 1881 Royal Commission on Mills and Factories which found conditions nothing short of revolting. "Workers were often herded in the lofts of buildings or in low, damp basements with artificial light in use during the whole day," according to historian Fred Landon. "Dangerous machinery was unprotected and steam engines and boilers were found in charge of boys, sometimes only thirteen or fourteen years of age." Some of what the commission found was "nauseating in the extreme," he concluded.

The Riel Rebellions and the building of a national railway occupied centre stage for much of the period between the 1881 report and the Royal Commission on the Relations of Labour and Capital that would close the decade in 1889. Little would truly change for the working class in the intervening eight years. Indeed, in his essay on the period, Bernard Ostry argues that, although some provincial laws were passed, the ruling federal Conservatives did not pass a single important measure on behalf of the industrial worker.

Fortunately, Donavon could not foresee how formidable his task would be. As the building, transportation, manufacturing and communications industries began to boom, thousands of workers moved to urban centres in the 1880s, encountering conditions of almost unthinkable hardship. Big cities like Toronto, Montreal and Hamilton suffered from a chronic lack of basic housing, sewage and water facilities. Employers kept wages low and hours long. Immigrant workers, arriving in floods through the government-backed immigration program, competed for jobs.

Acutely aware of these conditions, the Knights promised to build a united front to combat the evils brought on by rapidly expanding free enterprise. The order provided a brilliant and sometimes radical program of social reforms. For a time, Donavon's *Advocate* was the perfect vehicle to bring that program to the doorstep of the new industrial worker.

The Knights wanted progressive labour laws such as lien acts to legally ensure that companies paid workers, factory acts to improve working conditions, and employer's liability acts to encourage companies to eliminate safety hazards. Debates over these and other proposals were carefully reported in the *Advocate*. Shorter working hours and improved working conditions had already become perennial issues of the young labour movement, and Donavon dutifully documented the arguments and gave credit to labour's advances. "By lawful agitation and persevering argument mechanics have caused Trade Unionism to become not alone a recognized part of our social system," he wrote, "but a power which politicians are forced to acknowledge."

However, after six months of publishing, Donavon's "sufficient faith in the honour and integrity of the workingman to know that they will cheerfully support us so long as we are true to our platform" had waned considerably. He appealed for greater support, based on the paper's record of exposing the "evils that bear against the working classes" and its aim to "secure justice to a class, that has no other mouthpiece in Canada." But the support was not forthcoming.

On March 8, 1883, he changed the paper's name to the *Wage-Worker*, announcing that it "will be fearless and independent . . . and will not truckle to any party." Ostensibly, the change was meant to help the editor "embrace the rights, the wrongs, and the material interests of all who earn their livelihood through the sweat of their brow." In truth, Donavon was staging a last ditch effort to rescue his failing weekly.

The end came on April 26, 1883, after exactly one year—52 issues. Claiming a lack of funds, though no shortage of love for the work, Donavon left his readers with the same message he had delivered in his first issue. He asked them to "eschew party politics, as well as parasites who sometimes under the guise of labour champions trade upon their kindnesses for the purpose of personal advancement and gain."

Donavon had helped lay the foundation of a new kind of labour movement, using the *Advocate* to identify a host of new ideas for change. Now he bowed out, leaving the task of promoting those ideas to another labour editor and a new paper as the country headed into another more serious depression.

The *Palladium of Labour* arrived boasting that it was the "only labour paper published in Canada." It was a slight exaggeration—Drummond's *Trades Journal* carried on publishing throughout the 1880s. But if it wasn't the only voice of the movement, the paper was destined to become the cream of 19th-century labour journals. It made its home in Hamilton, which 20 years earlier had seen the founding of Isaac Buchanan's *Workingman's Journal*. But in philosophy, the *Palladium* was light years away from Buchanan's compromising views on the necessity for co-operation between capital and labour.

The *Palladium* began life as the *Labour Union* on January 13, 1883, stating that it was "A Weekly Journal Devoted to the Interests of All Classes of Labour." By August, editor William H. Rowe had changed the name to the *Palladium*. The slogan changed as well. Now it was to be devoted "to the Interests of Workingmen and Working Women." The upfront recognition of women workers was the first of many breakthroughs for the second Canadian Knights paper.

From the start, Rowe broke new ground in offering a two-cent Saturday morning tabloid. He vastly increased circulation from the *Advocate's* several hundred to a press run of 5,000 to 7,000. Advertisers in the booming steel industry town gladly purchased 40 per cent of the eight pages, a feat never to be repeated by other 19th-century labour papers. He gave a voice to the most outspoken champions of labour's cause, providing a major forum for the debate of social problems and the open advocacy of socialist solutions. Rowe also boldly pioneered the use of muckraking techniques to expose wrongdoing in the factories and the legislatures of the land.

Little is known of the *Palladium* editor's personal background. He was the son of a wool merchant from Cornwall, England, who moved his family to the United States in 1866, then to Canada two years later. The elder William "met with fair success" in the wool and commission business under the company name of Berryman and Rowe. At his death of tuberculosis in 1884, he left five daughters and young William as his only son.

Rowe Jr. teamed up with a journalist named George W. Taylor for the *Palladium's* first few months, but the "part proprietor" soon moved on to the *Detroit Free Press* and a career in commercial journalism. Perhaps he was put off by Rowe's highly opinionated attitude or his intemperance. Whatever the reason, it fell to Rowe to "support the cause of the Productive Industry, by making knowledge a standpoint for action, and industrial, moral worth, not wealth, the true standard of individual and national greatness."

Like the *Advocate*, the *Palladium* was non-partisan and non-sectarian. Its cause was "the cause of the People." Its mission was to "Spread the Light; to expose the inequalities of distribution by which the few are enriched at the expense of the many." The new paper was cocky and proud and its editor was driven in his role as labour reformer and social advocate. But Rowe needed help from someone who shared his belief in trade union principles and possessed the journalistic skills to make the pages of the *Palladium* come alive. Most important, he needed a writer who would attack the greatest enemy of social justice—the monopoly—with the determination of a bull terrier. That person was a Toronto journalist named Thomas Phillips Thompson, a man whose contribution to 19th-century social reform cannot be overestimated.

Under the pen-name Enjolras, appropriately lifted from Victor Hugo's famous novel *Les Miserables*, Thompson lit into the capitalist system with a vengeance. His front-page column brought readers a weekly dose of his often humorous, sometimes bitter views on every subject under the sun. Enjolras set the pace of labour journalism in the early 1880s, leaving a long trail of top-notch arguments against the monopolists and against the system that impoverished his Knights readers.

"It is the spirit of society which needs to be radically and fundamentally regenerated," Thompson wrote in a typical column. "It is not in this reform or that, so much as in the spread of generous sympathies and the encouragement of the better impulses of humanity which are now systematically stifled and crushed out by false teaching that the social condition of mankind will be improved."

Although Thompson growled at governments and howled against employers and even his fellow labour advocates, the monopolists were his chief target. "Were it not for land monopoly," he wrote, "none of these villainous schemes by which the capitalist devil-fish draws within its capricious clutch the earnings of the toiling millions would be possible." The schemes he attacked included railway and stock gambling, political corruption, wheat and coal owners and manufacturing rings, increased immigration and money monopolies, to name but a few.

Rowe vented his frustrations with the system by publishing the writings of Enjolras, but there were other columns, some no doubt written by the editor, that also bashed the system. "Our Social Club" was one. Another, "Twixt Hammer and Anvil," issued an early call for nationalization, arguing that "private corporations for quasi-public purposes have outlived their usefulness and scandalously abused their prerogatives. The sooner the Government takes charge of the railroads, the telegraphs, the currency and the insurance business the better."

Earlier labour editors had proposed a worker-owner alliance, co-operatives and leglislative reform as answers to improving the lot of working families. Thompson called for nothing short of social revolution. In a moment of unrestrained joy, he wrote: "It is coming, yes, the revolution is coming! . . . The light is breaking, the clouds are passing. Hail to the rising sun of Freedom." Earlier he had written in more cautious terms that "we do not advocate Revolution, but at the rate at which the concentration of wealth and its natural consequences—the increase of poverty—are proceeding, it is apparently the inevitable outcome."

The revolution was a long way off, but Thompson accurately named the increase in poverty as the biggest threat of rampant free-enterprise industrialization. Rowe regularly published items on the poor. "The overseers of the poor in some of the New Brunswick parishes annually sell the aged and decrepit paupers to those who are willing to keep them at the cheapest figure for the year," one item reported. But the *Palladium* hardly needed to go so far afield to find images of destitution. There were plenty to go around in Ontario.

Curbing monopolies and overthrowing the expanding capitalist economy was clearly the only way to end such inhuman poverty, Rowe and Thompson argued. They had little time for mere reformists or puritanical proposals from social institutions such as the church. As Donavon had suggested in the *Advocate*, Christian organizations would do far better to devote "a portion of their time in persuading many of our close fisted bosses to pay a living wage to their male and female employees."

In one of many attacks on the clergy's role in helping the poor, Rowe followed suit, declaring that "evil is the legitimate outcome of private land ownership and the competitive system." However, the *Palladium* did regard the religious press with some respect, saying that it was "a source of gratification to labour reformers to know that not only the pulpit but the religious press as well, are rapidly falling into line . . . [with respect to] the great question of the relation between Labour and capital, competition and co-operation."

Although the Knights sympathized with the temperance movement, they considered it another half-measure. The abolition of monopolies, rather than prohibition, was the key message of the *Palladium*. And Rowe and Thompson wasted no time informing readers that the most evil monopoly of all was the banking system, which was "nothing more nor less than legalized robbery."

The solution to the problem was clear. But how would it come about? First, the workers needed to build strong unions and place labour representatives in the legislatures. "The ultimate goal of the Labour Reform movement is the establishment of an industrial democracy on the ruins of the present capitalistic system," Rowe wrote in a cautionary note reminiscent of Donavon's strident anti-political days. "No two-penny-half-penny measure such as the politicians promise, can or ought to satisfy Labour Reformers."

Taking Donavon's lead, the *Palladium* editor was suspicious of political parties. But he also recognized the value of legislative change and he urged support for labour candidates who could introduce progressive amendments to the Ontario Factories Act.

One of the main goals of the agitation for the passage or amendment of factory acts was to limit the use of child labour. Earlier, Donavon had explained why the "demoralizing" practice had to end: "The employment of ten or twelve year old children helps destroy homes," he editorialized, "as they frequently find, after a short stay in the factory, more congenial spirits than in the home circle." The *Advocate* had also exposed "the employment of little girls in some of the cotton, woolen and silk mills" in one front-page item.

Rowe, too, rarely missed an opportunity to expose the damaging effects of this "morally, socially, and industrially wrong" practice, whereby young children were exploited and adult unemployment was perpetuated by employers using children to do adult work.

To assist labour candidates in pressing for tough new labour laws, Rowe employed many journalistic tactics. He published detailed accounts of injuries on the job, providing strong emotional ammunition in the political arena. One item lamented the sad fate of young Fred Hanly, whose hand was badly mangled by a cotton mill machine before his 14th birthday. The *Palladium* editor also introduced what may have been the first attempt at muckraking in a Canadian labour journal. Hiring an unnamed investigator to uncover alleged employer abuses in cotton mills, the weekly soon reported that "children as young as nine and ten years of age are kept at work for twelve hours each day."

Donavon had reported in the *Advocate* that the Knights wanted "to secure for both sexes equal pay for equal work." "Where a woman can perform certain duties as well as men," one article said, "there is no earthly reason why she should receive less wages than the sterner sex." Another item addressed "sister workers" with this call to arms: "You have been trampled upon and dragged in the dirt too long already. If you do not make a move for reform in your own behalf, you must expect to remain in the servile condition in which you are at present."

Rowe also backed the equal pay for equal work movement and campaigned for over-all equality. As he saw it, legislation was desperately needed to correct the generally inferior treatment of women workers, especially domestic servants and "factory girls." He supported laws such as the Carlton Act meant to protect these young women from employers who might make sexual advances or induce them into a life of prostitution.

Thompson, who had long been a champion of women's rights, wrote, "the right of woman to be regarded in all matters of citizenship and all relations between the government and the people as the equal of man can hardly be denied by any clear-sighted and consistent Labour Reformer."

Lobbying for legislative solutions to social problems was an important function of the movement. Although the Knights promoted relief and mutual benefit societies, agitation for higher wages was a more significant part of the strategy for achieving social change. Donavon first explained the logic: "Let the merchants, manufacturers, and others pay a good wage for a day's work, not a mere pittance to keep body and soul together, but sufficient for a man to keep his family respectably upon, and enable him to lay up a little each year for old age, then, and not until then, will the true remedy be found."

Rowe agreed. Everyone in the working family, especially old people, would benefit from better wages, pensions and social insurance laws. The *Palladium* stressed that "No man whose best years have been spent in useful and honourable toil . . . ought to be left destitute during the latter years of his life." The paper called for a tax on the wealthy to help support retired workers and suggested that monopoly was at fault for not allowing the elderly to live "beyond the reach of want."

On the related issue of weekly pay days, the "Twixt Hammer and Anvil" columnist noted that they were "one of the civilizing agencies of the future." They were needed to slow the use of credit and therefore save workers from falling into unending debt and eventual poverty.

Shorter hours of work were crucial to lowering unemployment, improving health and living conditions. The *Advocate* and the *Palladium* campaigned for an eight-hour day just as vigorously as the *Ontario Workman* supported the nine-hour movement in the previous decade. The eight-hour day was a *cause célèbre* of the 1880s, especially in the United States where the famous Haymarket riot in Chicago led to the hanging of allegedly anarchist union leaders who advocated the shorter work day. "To prolong labour beyond that period is commercially unprofitable, economically illogical, and morally wrong," Rowe argued.

Rowe and Thompson believed that the election of labour candidates would result in progressive changes in all social areas. But the success rate of such candidates was not encouraging. They therefore supported other methods of promoting change as well, such as co-operation, a solution proposed by earlier labour papers. Thompson prompted workers to "make the same sacrifices and show the same spirit in co-operative experiments—even if they don't look very promising—as they do in connection with strikes and lockouts and boycotts."

The Knights did not favour strikes and boycotts as the means to settle disputes. Instead, they advocated compulsory arbitration. However, despite the official stance, the boycott and strike were often used, and the *Advocate* and the *Palladium* gave ample coverage to such activities at home and abroad.

Whatever else was needed to right the wrongs created by the industrial system, the Knights saw education as a key social tool for aiding the masses to achieve their ends. But like other issues the order embraced, the education issue was a complex one. "If wage-workers are ever to become a powerful body for their own good," Donavon wrote, "an organized body that will not be carried away by artful and designing men—a body who are willing to think for themselves, and not follow blindly a false scent laid by tricksters—a body capable of sternly demanding justice, and accepting no compromise—it is their bounden duty to read, to study, to think, concerning their own interests. It is their duty to EDUCATE themselves."

Donavon felt education was a first step toward "liberation" from the "wage-thieving employers," but his enthusiasm didn't extend to support for the government-sponsored education system, which he thought to be "a vicious one, inevitably leading to the worst results. The persistent cramming of the poor little mind till the over-worked brain reels, cannot but be productive of evil."

The *Palladium* justified its support for compulsory school attendance by saying that it would give more jobs to the unemployed, with cheap child labour forced into school during the day. But, as the "Twixt Hammer and Anvil" columnist remarked, "Although we have a Compulsory Education Act on our statutes, no effort is made to enforce it." Those parents who did abide by the law were no doubt shocked to read in the *Palladium* that the "idea of educating is to break the child's will." The paper further suggested that "There are brutes to-day employed in educating our youth who themselves require education." Still, education was the most effective way to sway public opinion and accelerate the "good time coming of social regeneration," Thompson proclaimed.

The *Palladium* and the *Advocate*, like most early labour supporters, expressed concern about the government's mass importation of Chinese immigrant workers as cheap labour. The language barrier made these workers difficult to organize, and Canadian workers felt their livelihoods were being threatened. Rowe used his weekly paper to mount a strong fight for the "anti-Chinese bill," which became law in 1885 and levied a $50 tax on every Chinese worker who landed in Canada and limited their number to one for "every fifty tons burden of the ship."

Only one other group felt the editorial sting of the *Palladium* or the *Advocate* as harshly—the commercial press and the workers who continued to buy it. Workers' support of the party press raised Donavon's blood pressure so high that when he ran out of his own words to blast them, he turned to the American labour press for help. "Workingmen howl against a 'subsidized press,' and newspapers devoted solely to the interest of capital, but continue to support them nevertheless," said an article reprinted from the Kansas City *New Argo*. "This is a rich farce, and is one of the many things which causes these journalistic manipulators to regard the railing of the people as unmeaning gas."

Rowe called mainstream journalists "beetle-browed ignora-muses" with "scarcely sufficient brains to appreciate even the gratification of their own selfish and idiotic malice." He warned workers that these "mercenaries" had no interest in the cause of working people beyond "its market value." Yet for all his criticism, it wasn't long before Rowe himself was also accused of undermining that same cause in favour of founding his own daily newspaper.

The *Palladium* editor had long wanted to start the labour movement's first daily, and had outlined plans for the daily *Labour Union* as early as 1882. He finally realized his dream at the end of 1886 with the founding of the *Evening Palladium*. The new paper preceded Britain's first labour daily, the *Daily Herald*, by 25 years, but it was a short-lived affair, lasting only a few issues. In one, Rowe took what turned out to be his parting shot at the daily competition. He appealed to local merchants to advertise, arguing that "rates are lower and cir-culation much larger than either of the two clumsy-looking blanket-sheets published in this city."

They were the same fighting words his readers had come to expect. After all, this wasn't the first time that the prince of Canadian labour papers had donned its armour in preparation for battle. In early 1884, a pair of bogus labour reformers named E.P. Morgan and Falconer L. Harvey rolled into Hamilton to wreak havoc and disorder among Knights members. The two set about disrupting the activities of the Hamilton assembly. They caused much dissension, were exposed as swindlers and quickly expelled from the order.

Soon after they arrived they got into a bitter scrap with the *Palladium* editor, who at one point went to jail for allegedly libelling Harvey. The two expelled Knights soon formed their own local union, the Universal Brotherhood of United Labour, and began to publish a rival paper called *Justice*. It was hardly a serious challenger to Rowe, but he was angered when the two partners in crime began soliciting the hard-earned dollars of subscribers and the precious few advertising accounts. *Justice* soon died and the two charlatans who had produced what the *Palladium* sarcastically called "that precious sheet" moved on. But Rowe had learned to keep his guard up in the precarious business of publishing a labour journal.

Such battles earned Rowe the respect and support of his Hamilton readers. Indeed, they were so pleased with the paper that in early 1885 the *Palladium* editor gleefully announced that he had ordered a "new double royal Campbell press" to meet the demands of the growing labour movement. Later that year, Rowe set up a Toronto edition of the *Palladium*, under the editorship of W.H. Bews.

But the future was not bright. The competition was encroaching on the provincial territory that Rowe had mapped out for the *Palladium*. It included a trio of rival Knights papers which, in the summer of 1886, became embroiled in an abusive editorial war about who was best serving the labour movement. Rowe was typically hot-headed in his approach, but the others rose to the bait. In a way, the bickering was an outward display of the divisive debates that were taking place within the order itself. The editors' war of words was an early warning signal that the end of the Knights' era was nigh.

5

The Knights' War of Words

The year 1886 was a watershed for the Knights of Labour. They were at the peak of their influence as a great upsurge of political activity swept Toronto. W.H. Howland, a Knights-endorsed mayoralty candidate, wooed the working-class vote and unseated the incumbent in an overwhelming victory. The win on the municipal scene spurred the movement to seek out other candidates for election provincially at Queen's Park and federally in Ottawa. Not since the early 1870s and the struggles of the nine-hour movement had there been such political fervour among labour advocates.

The political stakes were high and Knights leaders soon divided into Grit and Tory camps. They began to publish labour journals at a furious rate, seeing them as a key resource in winning labour's vote. By the spring of 1886, at least three new Knights weeklies were launched, and they were soon engaged in an editorial fight to the death.

Daniel J. O'Donoghue began publishing the *Labour Record* in Toronto on May 1, 1886. The former Ottawa printer circulated his first tabloid issue that spring Saturday, promising that it would "ever be found doing battle for the cause of justice and humanity." O'Donoghue, having won labour's first seat in the Ontario legislature back in 1874, was a key figure in Ontario labour circles. Clearly, he had the clout to back up his boast that the *Record* would be "a truthful index of the views of organized labour on all questions affecting the public welfare, whether of a moral, social, political or municipal character."

On Wednesday, May 12, George Wrigley's *Canada Labour Courier* hit the streets in St. Thomas, Ontario. It was printed in a larger format than most labour weeklies, but its aims echoed those of other official Knights journals. Wrigley claimed that his paper would be "ready at all times to champion the rights of the labour classes, without regard to sex, colour, religion or nationality."

Later that year, Knights in London, Ontario, requested permission at a general assembly to start a co-operative newspaper under the auspices of the order. The request was turned down; southern Ontario hardly seemed ready for yet another labour newspaper. Already the existing Knights organs were finding it difficult to co-exist.

On Saturday, May 15, Toronto workers had picked up the first copies of the *Canadian Labour Reformer*. With Alexander Whyte Wright as the editor and R.L. Simpson and R. Kingsmill as managers, its arrival set the scene for the coming battle royale among competing Knights papers.

The *Reformer* was unusual in comparison to the others—12 pages in a magazine format—and it cost a whopping five cents. But the readers didn't seem to mind. A few months before, Wright had bought the failing Toronto edition of the *Palladium of Labour*, whose Hamilton parent continued to be the scourge of anti-labour forces. Now he bragged that Toronto subscribers to the defunct Toronto *Palladium* had stayed with the *Reformer* and indeed "far more than doubled" in number. A reader from Brantford, Ontario, commented: "I am pleased to see the first number of the *Labour Reformer* launched forth on the turbulent waters of labour journalism with her sails set to the breeze and her helm well down . . . .Several complain about the width of her reading columns, but I suppose that is a matter of taste."

The waters were indeed turbulent for Wright. Although the paper's slogan was "We demand all the reform that justice can ask for and all the justice that reform can give," Wright was a dedicated Tory. His notion of reform was questioned by a labour movement that had seen little in the way of progressive social change from the ruling Conservative Party.

Some claimed he was merely an opportunist, a charlatan not above engaging in underhanded political activities. A letter to Sir John A. Macdonald in 1884 lent credibility to these speculations. In 1883, he had concocted a plan to buy Rowe's financially troubled *Labour Union* (later *Palladium*) with Tory money. Now he asked the Tory leader to put up $4,000 to buy the troubled Hamilton *Palladium*, which had momentarily ceased publication.

"My plan," he wrote the prime minister in 1884, "is to have a labour paper started which will be made the organ of the Knights of Labour and perhaps the Trades and Labour Council. Put it in the form of a joint stock company allotting a minority of the stock to the more active and prominent members of the labour organizations, thus identifying them with the paper without running the risk of actually letting them get control of it."

He told Macdonald that he hoped to gain the confidence of workers by producing the paper "on a purely labour platform, even antagonizing the Conservative Party where it could be done harmlessly but whenever opportunity offered putting in a word where it would do good." The little cabinet-maker was no doubt thrilled by Wright's letter, as he recalled his compromising loan to the *Ontario Workman* of 10 years before.

The takeover fell through when the Hamilton Knights set up a co-operative to keep the paper in labour's hands. But Wright's plan exposed his tight Tory connections and the party's strong desire to control the labour vote. The editor's Conservative ties went back to the early 1870s when he had taken up woolen manufacturing in several southwestern Ontario towns around his birthplace of Elmira. He was a member of the Orange Lodge, and had served with the Ontario Rifles Company, which had helped put down the Riel Rebellion of 1870. Soon after, he moved into journalism, spending short stints as editor of the Guelph *Herald*, the Orangeville *Sun* and the Stratford *Herald*. The editing experience prepared him to take over the *National*, a Toronto political weekly founded by H.E. Smallpiece and Phillips Thompson in 1874. In its pages, Wright sung the praises of the producer ideology and currency reform, causes that *Workingman's Journal* editor Isaac Buchanan had championed back in the mid-1860s.

When the *National* folded in 1880, Wright quickly founded the *Commonwealth* and set about campaigning for the Tory seat in West Toronto. After his bid failed, he closed the new paper and moved on to become secretary of the Ontario Manufacturer's Association and an active member of the Canadian Currency Reform League. Along the way, he had also developed a keen interest in labour issues.

The *Reformer* gave Wright the ideal vehicle to reach the hearts and minds of the swelling Knights membership. With his considerable journalistic talent, it quickly became a reasoned voice for Knights-style social advocacy. Members of a Knights assembly in West Lambton were so impressed with Wright's abilities that they nominated the Tory labour advocate to run for a seat in the Ontario legislature in late 1886.

He shared the Knights view that labour disputes were only symptoms of a "deep-seated disease in our social system," and urged adherence to the principles of labour reform. "We have to face a long, stern and arduous conflict," he argued in his opening editorial. Knights had "to do our part manfully through good and evil report, in prosperity and adversity, having in view the ultimate triumph of our principles, which will come surely as there is a God in Heaven or an innate sense of justice and right in the great heart of humanity. This, rather than the more transitory object, should be the aim of every true Labour Reformer."

Electing labour candidates, including himself, was clearly a priority if labour was to achieve its goals. And, like Rowe and Thompson, Wright saw monopolies as the cause of the "worst evils of the present social condition." The paper's first front cover, for example, carried the headline, "Strangled by Monopoly," and sported a full-page illustration of an adult and two children struggling with a snake-like railway, referring to the streetcar monopoly in Toronto.

In a later article, Wright blamed land monopoly for the adverse effects of technological change. "It is monopoly of the land and the money that enables the few to use machinery to cheapen labour and further enrich themselves," he wrote, adding that mechanization should benefit workers with shorter hours and higher wages. Poverty was an obvious by-product of the capitalist system, he argued, "and on thinking more deeply it will become clear that but for this system actual poverty could not exist."

Wright's arguments were so convincing at times that it seemed incongruous that he would associate with the political party so clearly in favour of that system. At any rate, he correctly identified monopoly as the key enemy and politics as the weapon to use against it. Earlier weapons, such as co-operation, would not solve the problem. It is a good thing, he told readers, "but they should avoid the mistake of supposing that it is the cure for the unfair distribution of wealth from which Labour suffers."

Political action was the ultimate solution for Wright. Only through labour representation in the legislature, for example, would an employers' liability act become a reality, ensuring workers of protection from health and safety hazards. Only such legislators could pressure governments to devise a social insurance plan. Advocating such reforms might also help the enterprising *Reformer* editor with a small business he ran on the side. Under his pen-name, Spokeshave, Wright said it was the government's duty to see that life insurance was within reach of all workers. Since the paper carried large advertisements offering subscribers an accidental death plan with "Funeral Benefit Insurance" for $25, critics accused Wright of using his position as an influential labour editor to feather his own nest.

Still, a government life insurance plan had been promised since as far back as 1879, so it was quite within the labour paper's mandate to press for its creation. Also, the Ancient Order of United Workmen in Orillia, Ontario, had been promoting life insurance through its journal, the *Canadian Workman*, since the late 1870s.

The insurance scheme may have had its shady side, but Wright was above board in his promotion of other Knights causes. Like Rowe and Donavon, he advocated legislative reforms that would benefit women. He strongly objected to the "absurd and unjust discriminations which restrict women to the least remunerative occupations and fix her receipts at a much lower figure than men can earn." He also rejected the exclusion of women from the vote and lashed out at wife beaters. "Woman beating," he wrote, "should be stamped out, and all respectable men should ostracise the miserable, cowardly wretch guilty of the offence."

Wright was not nearly so generous with his sympathy when it came to immigrant labour. One item of subtle racist humour illustrated the point: " 'Will Chinamen eat rats?,' asked a small boy. 'That depends,' said his father. 'If they are clean, decent rats, perhaps, but even a heathen Chinese will refuse scab rats'." As to charitable attempts to help immigrant workers, Wright noted that "quite as much good might be done in looking after our own destitute poor." The labour movement, angered by the government's immigration policy, often responded by denigrating the Chinese workers. Wright felt compelled to support the call for the protection of Canadian workers' jobs in a similar manner. In most other cases, however, he steered readers toward sympathy with the underdog, a trait displayed by all the Knights papers publishing at the time.

As Wright was perfecting his skills as a labour journalist, other Knights organs had begun to spread out across the land. Winnipeg Knights welcomed the *Call* which the *Palladium* called "a neatly printed 'spicy' twenty column weekly." The *Call* editor warned "scoundrels who rob and plunder" that his paper "will prove a terror." The *Reformer* expressed surprise at the appearance of the *Winnipeg Industrial News*, but welcomed the "well-written" newcomer. Further west, there was rumour of a Calgary paper called the *Northwest Call*. Vancouver Knights had brought out an organ to support labour candidates, and Vancouver Island workers were reading the *Victoria Industrial News*.

Despite the encouraging comments by Wright and other Ontario Knights editors, by early 1886 a tight labour publishing market had developed. The *Reformer* in Toronto and the *Palladium* in Hamilton vied for provincial and even national labour newspaper status, while the other Knights papers nipped at their heels. The competition from within the movement meant even tighter budgets for the struggling papers, as readers chose one labour paper over another. It also meant that the various political rivalries which had simmered for years began to surface as labour editors attempted to discredit their competitors. The fight for allegiance couldn't help but spill on to the pages of the labour press; soon it blew into a full-scale labour press war.

By the mid-1880s, the labour press would also face heavy competition from outside the movement in central Canada. Despite a population of one and a half million workers, labour editors soon learned that the actual paying readership was very small. Even then, it was hard work to attract and hold their attention. Workers might read something that was already in the home, but they seldom went in search of literary material. This was a source of much frustration which often led labour editors and leaders to chastise trade unionists. "Out of 140 Labour papers started within the last two years, one-half of them have gone under," chided American labour radical Richard Trevellick in a tirade typical of movement editors. "[They were] starved to death, and by you."

In Toronto, the market grew even more competitive with the arrival of weeklies such as Goldwin Smith's the *Week* (changed

from the *Bystander*) and *Monetary Times,* an organ of the pro-
tectionist Canada First Movement. Both drew much fire from
the labour press. The *Palladium* once joked that if the *Week*
wasn't any better than the *Bystander,* it ought to be spelled
"Weak." In fact, Smith, also well known for his views against
women's suffrage, had become almost as infamous an arch-
villain to labour as the *Globe*'s George Brown.

The daily press was also invading the huge market represented by the working classes by offering often sensational,
sometimes probing coverage of social issues. Such coverage
was so appealing to readers that the labour press often reprinted
the material alongside sharp criticisms of the "monopoly" or
"capitalistic press."

London *Advertiser* founder and Knights sympathizer James
Cameron began to shift the *Globe*'s anti-labour emphasis when
he became editor in 1882. And papers like the Toronto *News,*
founded by Edmund Ernest Sheppard, and the Bobcaygeon
Independent became defiant supporters of labour's cause. Both
papers prided themselves on serving the workers and their
families through exposés of wrongdoing, either corporate or
political, and strong editorials aimed at reforming the social
system. As historian Russell Hann shows in his exhaustive
essay on the *News,* it not only reflected many Knights views,
but what made it truly different from the party press was its
"enunciation of a political course that was clearly independent
of Grittism or Toryism."

Ironically, the rise of the commercial dailies also had some
positive effects on the pioneer labour press. "When workers
began to organize and to launch their own journals to advance
their cause, they might find in their own ranks a handful of
learned artisans and the odd self-taught journalist trained at
the printer's case to staff their papers," Hann writes. "More
often, they relied heavily upon sympathetic journalists who
became labour's intellectuals."

But whereas disillusioned journalists helped the labour
press develop, the popular evening press drew the working-
class reader away from the labour weeklies. The *Palladium* saw
the double-edged sword. It hailed the "sympathy with the
cause of labour reform" displayed by the *News* and a few other
dailies, but argued that labour papers "are the school books
that labour needs, and [they are] absolutely essential to advancement. These independent guerilla labour papers, scattered

throughout the country, are more reliable than any central organ can be."

Part of the appeal of the dailies, once a party press aligned with the Tories or the Whigs, was their transformation into so-called "people's journals," the forerunners of today's daily press. These were "business enterprises, which their proprietors expected would produce a large advertising revenue," notes media historian Paul Rutherford. "Consequently the papers were designed to appeal not only to professionals and businessmen but also to clerks, workingmen, women and the young."

The people's journals were so intent on absorbing the working-class readership that they openly attacked the establishment and even "championed the cause of the masses," Rutherford writes. "Before most of their contemporaries, these papers perceived that the political and economic institutions of the community sometimes worked against the happiness of the lower classes. Much of their attention was fixed on the plight of the workingman and his family."

Papers like the Montreal *Star*, the Ottawa *Citizen* and later the Toronto *Telegram* saw themselves as purveyors of objective news and struck out against the stodgy style and partisan politics of the party press. Borrowing from its penny press counterparts in the United States, this new breed of newspaper pretended to be crusaders under the banner of journalism for the ordinary citizen. But they were not above cashing in on the lucrative working-class market by publishing lurid crime reports and news of bizarre events in exotic lands. New technologies and journalistic conventions gave the commerical press an indisputable edge over the financially strapped labour press in attracting and influencing workers and their families. As historian Greg Kealey notes, "The presence of a labour press and of the new popular papers forced some of the established newspapers to rethink many of their attitudes, and even their space allocations. Thus the *Globe* invited O'Donoghue to contribute a weekly labour column."

Even more threatening competition was posed by weekly magazines, which offered some of the same fare as the labour press and therefore could bite into the activist readership, the small but solid subscription base of the labour papers. The Toronto *Truth*, for example, or the *Social Reformer* (issued irregularly), or the widely respected satirical weekly *Grip* were all sympathetic to the people the labour press pledged to serve. They offered a variety of reading material and did not have the sometimes hindering affiliation with a labour body.

There were also the family, farm and ethnic publications, the religious and temperance press, as well as consumer magazines. *Saturday Night*, for example would be founded in 1887 by Toronto *News* publisher E. E. Sheppard. There was even an openly atheist press which included *Secular Thought*, a Toronto paper published by Charles Watts.

This crowded and competitive media market place formed the backdrop to the long summer of 1886 when the four Knights editors confronted each other in an unusual display of internecine warfare.

The *Palladium* fired the first salvo, opening up both barrels against O'Donoghue's *Labour Record*: "The only thing we know to its detriment is the suspicious circumstances that the *Spectator* praises its 'judgment and discretion' and considers it 'an admirable Labour organ'." Never missing a chance to smear the daily press, Rowe added, "We hope the *Record*'s course will not be such as to deserve the praises of the capitalistic press, and doubt not that as opportunity arises it will do its best to earn that malignant hatred and abuse from the champions of monopoly which is the surest indication that a Labour Reformer is doing his duty."

Two weeks later, Wrigley was caught using boiler plate matter (pre-designed and packaged pages) at the *Canada Labour Courier*. Rowe charged that the press-ready pages were produced by "rats" and "sometimes girls, working like slaves." Chinese "cheap labour" was also supposedly involved and that was the kiss of death given labour's stand against the immigrant workers. The *Palladium*'s "Twixt Hammer and Anvil" column dumped salt in the wound with this comment: "Hologaugus is Tuscarora for 'no good'. We have come to the painful conclusion that some of the alleged Labour journals which have sprung into existence like unhealthy growths are hologaugus."

The *Courier* was quick to respond, devoting "four columns of its space to telling readers what kind of paper the *Palladium* is." The Hamilton weekly shot back with: "Evidently the *Courier* is hankering to have us kick it into notoriety. But we don't intend to do it, except at the regular advertising rates."

O'Donoghue, a Liberal, and his *Labour Record* came in for more badgering later that summer for failing to respond to a *Palladium* call for editorial comment on A.B. Ingram's acceptance of the Tory-backed nomination as the St. Thomas labour candidate in the riding of West Elgin. Rowe also went after O'Donoghue for failing to criticize the Ontario government's immigration policy in an article lambasting a similar policy of the federal government. "Why does a paper professing to be published in the interest of labour, make fish of one and flesh of the other administration in a case where both are so clearly to blame?" Rowe wanted to know.

Wrigley's *Canada Labour Courier*, which Rowe characterized as an "insignificant concern in St. Thomas," also failed to speak out on the Ingram issue. In fact, Wrigley had lashed out at Ingram during the election campaign, telling readers that the candidate had renounced his labour views and was backing the Conservatives. Local Knights came to Ingram's defence, demanding that Wrigley apologize publicly for his attacks on the Tory-leaning candidate. The *Courier* editor refused. The *Reformer*, too, felt the heat from the *Palladium*'s big guns, until Wright quickly took what Rowe thought to be a "sound and sensible" position on the Ingram question.

By autumn of 1886, the *Reformer* got into the baiting game in a big way when it attacked the *Courier* for bitterly lashing out at the *Palladium* and the *Record*. Apparently, Wright did not like Wrigley's explanation of how the *Palladium* had "exerted its pernicious influence" on the *Record* in the matter of Ingram's candidacy. "We sincerely trust that the *Courier* will adopt a more moderate tone in criticizing journals which should be, and are, co-labourers in the cause," Wright noted.

The *Courier*, ever ready for a fight, charged the *Reformer* with political partisanship. Wright defended his paper as "an honest, earnest worker in the cause of oppressed humanity," which had suffered a "wholly unprovoked attack." Noting that workers were forced to pay for the *Courier* through Knights dues because it was an official organ, whereas the *Reformer* charted its path unaided in the precarious market place, Wright concluded with this thoughtful remark: "We believe the object of a Labour journal should be to report things as they really are, unmask iniquities, uproot prejudices, expose falsehoods, advocate genuine reform, and assist the toiling masses to attain

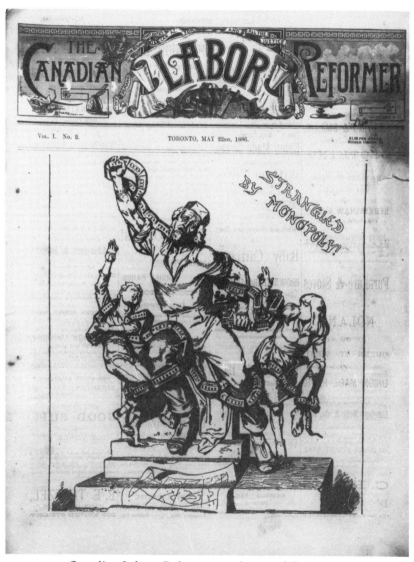

Canadian Labour Reformer (Archives of Ontario).

Workingman's Jour-nal founder Isaac Buchanan (National Archives of Canada/ C-23083).

Trades Journal editor Robert Drummond (Nova Scotia Archives).

Labour Record editor Daniel J. O'Donoghue, the father of the Canadian labour movement (National Archives of Canada/ C-43281).

Citizen and Country editor George Wrigley depicted as a dandy in the *Canada Farmer's Sun*, March 6, 1894 (Archives of Ontario).

Phillips Thompson
a few years before
joining the *Palla-
dium of Labour* as its
popular political
columnist, Enjolras
(*American Punch*,
July 1879).

Labour Advocate edi-
tor Phillips Thomp-
son, the most pro-
lific of all pioneer
labour journalists,
as an older man
(National Archives
of Canada/C-38584).

Toronto *Industrial Banner* editor James Simpson (*Working People*, Desmond Morton and Terry Copp).

Winnipeg *People's Voice* editor C.C. Steuart on front page of September 16, 1898, edition of the *Voice*.

The Winnipeg *Voice* staff with editor Puttee and child circa 1897 (Manitoba Archives).

THE
ONTARIO WORKMAN.

THE PALLADIUM
of Labor
A JOURNAL DEVOTED TO THE INTERESTS OF WORKINGMEN AND WORKINGWOMEN.

The Industrial Banner.
PUBLISHED BY THE TRADES AND LABOR COUNCIL.

FOR THE RIGHT,
AGAINST THE WRONG!

FOR THE WEAK,
AGAINST THE STRONG!

THE LABOR ADVOCATE.

We Demand all the Reform that Justice can ask for, and all the Justice that Reform can give.

TORONTO, CANADA, DECEMBER 12, 1890.

Vol. I.—No. 2.

$1.50 a Year, in Advance.
Single Copy, 5 Cents.

The banners of pioneer labour newspapers ranged from very ornate to plain (Canada Labour Library).

a higher degree of intellectual, moral and social development than they have yet enjoyed."

The labour papers should have aspired to these ideals, instead of battling among themselves, and the clarity of the statement should have had a sobering effect on all concerned. But by early 1887, Wright and O'Donoghue were back into a public mudslinging match provoked by their deep political differences. Eventually the *Reformer* won out.

The end of the in-fighting came none too soon for the weary working-class readers who wanted to support the labour press. The issue of supporting labour candidates in elections was a crucial one, but the debate became far too personal, with both O'Donoghue and Wright intent on impressing American Knights leader T.V. Powderly with their political savvy. Wright came out the winner, but it is a wonder that Canadian workers did not completely wash their hands of the lot and shift allegiance to papers which stuck closer to the issues. Perhaps some workers did just that, as the following lament published by Wright would suggest.

"We imagine the editors of those [labour] papers, sitting in a cheerless room, working night and day in a cause that seems hopeless," the *Reformer* editor wrote. "Their office is on the third storey in a back room. The type is old and battered. The everlasting question is: 'Where will the money come from to buy paper, and pay the printers and postage?' Their whole soul is in the cause they advocate. They send out samples time and again to those for whom they are labouring, but few postal orders or registered letters come."

The *Reformer* outlived all its adversaries, becoming the organ of Knights District Assemblies 61 and 125. It, too, failed in 1888 but made a brief comeback under the editorship of Phillips Thompson in 1889. The Hamilton *Palladium* had ceased to publish by late 1886, after its brief run as a daily, and its editor Rowe seems to have fallen into obscurity. O'Donoghue took a government post with the Ontario Bureau of Industries and later became the country's first fair-wage officer. Wrigley later resurfaced as the editor of numerous journals, including the *Farmers' Sun* and *Citizen and Country*, a socialist weekly of which we will hear more later. Wright moved to Philadelphia where he became Powderly's personal adviser and editor of the American Knights' official paper, the *Journal of United Labour*. He returned to Ontario in 1893, after the Knights had almost disbanded, and two years later was appointed to a royal commission investigating sweat shop labour for Ontario's Conservative government. He went on to edit a Tory labour paper in Toronto and became vice-chairman of the Ontario Workmen's Compensation Board.

At the decade's end, the Knights' position in favour of arbitration, their dislike of strikes, and their politics in general no longer satisfied the more radical elements of the labour intelligentsia. A different style of unionism was on the rise, with the increasing consolidation of union strength under the Trades and Labour Congress.

Still, the impending demise of the Knights did not spell the complete disappearance of papers inspired by the order. The fact that there had been little evidence of any real change during the previous decade only spurred editors like Thompson to march into the Gay Nineties with an even more single-minded goal: the sweet victory of socialism. For the first time, the man historians have called the father of the Canadian labour press would have his chance to press for that goal at the helm of his own labour paper.

6

Thompson's Last Stand

By the end of the 1880s, the Knights of Labour were showing deepening signs of decay. With the new decade came increasingly harsh social realities which called for a new vision of social change from the labour movement. As the Trades and Labour Congress became more stable, the Knights continued their decline. With the help of their outspoken journals, the Knights had built a mighty legion of workers and added new spirit to the youthful Canadian labour movement. But bruised from internal battles and battered by the thankless task of courting a largely unsupportive readership, the editors of these journals scattered to various corners of the movement. The task of keeping the Knights message alive fell to one man.

Thomas Phillips Thompson's career as a radical labour journalist had already spanned two decades when he began publishing the last, and some say greatest, of the Knights papers, the *Labour Advocate*, on a cool December Friday in 1890. If the announcements of the new Toronto weekly's arrival seemed to dwell on the status of its founding editor, it was with good reason.

Thompson's family had come to Canada in the late 1850s from Newcastle-on-Tyne, England, where Thompson was born in 1843. By the 1880s Thompson had become the outspoken labour commentator of his day on social issues, and his boundless energy and dedication to the cause were legion. Some of those qualities would rub off on a grandson by the name of Pierre Berton who would later take up the pen on writing crusades of his own.

Trained as a lawyer, he had taken up journalism after only a brief period in practice. He had tried his hand at humour in a weekly *Mail* column under the pen-name Jimuel Briggs, D.B. (for Dead Beat), from Coboconk University. The experience sharpened his political wit, thus preparing him for a career as one of the most prolific practitioners of radical Canadian journalism. In 1874, he and H.E. Smallpiece co-founded the *National*, a political and economic journal which served up propaganda for Sir John A. Macdonald's National Policy.

Thompson also sought an allegiance with the Canada First movement and its journal the *Nation*. To that end, he promised *National* readers lots of "snap and spice—vim and vigour." "Untrammelled by journalistic conventionalities and bound by no slavish deference to English or American models it seeks to promote the growth of a healthy, indigenous Canadian literature, racy of soil, and reflecting Canadian sentiment." But by the 1880s Thompson had broken with the Canada Firsters, who opposed trade unionism, and become an advocate of labour's cause.

He had also worked on several newspapers, starting at the St. Catharines *Post* where he covered the Fenian Raids of 1866, then moving to the Toronto *Telegram* and the Toronto *Mail*. He was a police reporter for the Toronto *Daily Telegraph* and had founded a paper called the *Daily City News*. In the early 1880s, he held a seat on the editorial board of the prestigious *Globe* and was assigned to cover events in Ireland. He had also journeyed to Boston to take up duties as literary editor of the *Evening Traveller*. While in the United States, he wrote for *American Punch* and the Boston *Courier*. In the mid-1880s, he had led the way on many important Knights issues through his influential Enjolras columns in the *Palladium of Labour*.

From his Enjolras writings Thompson pieced together his book, *The Politics of Labour*, written in 1887. Henry George, who argued in *Progress and Poverty* that land monopoly was the main cause of social problems, was instrumental in getting the book published. He had a great impact on Thompson, as did Edward Bellamy, whose utopian novel *Looking Backward* appeared in 1888 and was an immediate sensation. The influence of Laurence Gronlund's 1884 book *The Co-operative Commonwealth* can also be seen in Thompson's work.

With the creation of the *Advocate*, Thompson finally got his own labour journal, and he wasted no time in turning the eight-page tabloid into his personal podium for promoting social reform and public dissent. The *Advocate* was the voice of labour's radical socialist fringe and a siren with which Thompson could guide his readers through a politicising journey not unlike his own, one which took him "from radical republicanism, to land and currency reform, to Bellamyite nationalism, to 'class-conscious' socialism," as historian John David Bell has pointed out.

The new paper, expensive at five cents a copy, was endorsed by the Toronto Trades and Labour Council and District Assembly 125 of the Knights. On the surface it reflected the stance of those official, rather conservative, labour bodies. Thompson believed in the Knights philosophy and he joined Local Assembly 7814 in 1886 so he could speak out on Knights issues at conventions of the Trades and Labour Congress. But the *Advocate* was also Thompson's personal diary, an open letter to radicals, in which the country's top labour intellectual pronounced on labour's political evolution. It was Thompson's instrument for steering labour toward socialism in the 1890s.

As historian Victor O. Chan has said, Thompson's "inspiring and enthusiastic editorship made a determined attempt to instill into the minds of the workmen that 'Socialism' alone was the solution of the labour problem." Bell concurs: "The originality of the *Labour Advocate*'s thought and its contribution to the development of the ideology of Canadian radicalism lay primarily in the completeness of its rejection of capitalism and economic individualism, and in its unprecedented exposition of an avowedly Socialist dogma."

For Thompson, then, the promotion of socialism had become the sole goal of his labour journalism. He used what the masthead described as a "Weekly Labour Reform Newspaper" to "demand all the reform that justice can ask for, and all the justice that reform can give." The slogan was borrowed from the defunct *Canadian Labour Reformer*, but Thompson had more claim to it than anyone else. After all, he had made a last-ditch attempt to resurrect the old Knights journal in 1889, and in a way the *Advocate* was meant to continue the work of the *Reformer*.

By 1890, Canadian workers had become more radical than ever before, thanks to a labour press that vigorously scrutinized every social institution. "Labour newspapers no longer merely demanded justice for workingmen within the established structure of society," according to historian Jane Elizabeth Masters. "Instead, the cry of the 1890s was for complete change in the entire social system." Thompson's *Labour Advocate* cried the loudest of all.

   With his long and varied career, Thompson had a well-trained eye for social injustice. In his opening editorial, he stated his intention to keep up the pressure on the cause of that injustice. The *Advocate* promised to "keep steadfastly in view the need of abolishing monopoly in all its forms." While it asserted the workers' right to control production for their own benefit, at the same time the paper urged reforms designed to "better the lot of the toiler and to lead up to more radical measures in the future."

   The *Advocate* supported the call for various local reforms and was especially in favour of public ownership of the Toronto street railway. But poverty of the mass of working people was Thompson's first concern and he analysed the situation in classic socialist terms. "In old times the workingman simply knew that he was poor while others were rich," he wrote. "Now he knows he is poor because others are rich." Thompson added a typical barb aimed at organized religions, saying that the worker "thought the social inequalities were due to chance or the mysterious ways of Providence. Now he knows that they are caused by robbery and injustice."

   As to the claims of the 1889 Royal Commission on the Relations of Labour and Capital that it had helped improve wages, benefits and working conditions, Thompson replied: "None of the suggestions of the commission have been put on the statute books." His view was that "the money laid out on this expensive job was worse than wasted, in as much as it was made the means of giving a soft job to a few political heelers in return for their influence at elections."

   The plight of women workers was his second major concern and Thompson took an unequivocal stand on the issue. For one thing, he hired the first woman labour editor for the *Advocate*'s women's page, a common feature of all labour newspapers at the time. Mrs. E. Day MacPherson made sure that women's issues got plenty of play and what didn't fit on her page would easily find a place amidst the less than two pages of advertisements the paper attracted. In the column "Casual Comments," a writer named George A. Howell using the pen-name Ben argued that "women should receive, in all cases where similar work is done, the same wages as are paid to men; anything less than this is injustice."

   On women's rights in general, the *Advocate* reported that women "agitate the subject of social reform by claiming a place in public functions, and are striving their utmost to regenerate the woman of to-day into a creature who shall have all the rights and responsibilities that hitherto have belonged to man." The paper gave fierce backing to women's suffrage, arguing that "woman without the ballot suffers from the discrimination against her sex and is forced to take lower wages for the same class of work for which men are better paid."

Even as late as 1890, child labour was a social issue of widespread concern which no labour editor could avoid, least of all the crusading Thompson. He reported that Quebec had passed amendments to its Factory Act "which will remedy some of the most glaring evils of child labour," and he gave credit to the "persistent agitation carried on by the labour organizations of Quebec." Housing shortages, health and safety and problems faced by the elderly were other concerns frequently covered in the *Advocate*.

Making the case for a national pension plan, Thompson deplored the fact that "old people who have never been convicted of crime but who are too feeble to work are sent by police magistrates and justices of the peace to jail, not from any feeling of compassion for them, but simply because a scandal would be created, and society would be shocked if they were allowed to starve on the streets or in their miserable garrets."

His ultimate solution to all of these problems was, of course, socialism. But, as implied by his opening editorial, Thompson saw some value in the various social reforms perennially touted by labour. They were part of the socialist recipe. Education, for example, was a key ingredient in the mix. One front-page cartoon, a rarity in the labour press up to this point, sported this caption: "When we get free books, we'll have real free schools, but not before." The single tax, stressing taxation of land monopolists, was blended in because it was "doing excellent work in breaking ground for Socialism, by causing people to think of the evils begotten by land monopoly and the way to remedy them." Temperance, shorter hours and social insurance were all included in the formula. A Toronto reader named Richard Lewis wrote to the *Advocate* to propose that an insurance tax be levied on the profits of mine owners "making ample provision for the families of the brave men who are killed in the discharge of duties."

None of these half-measures held any real meaning for Thompson, who was increasingly convinced that the "approaching revolution will probably be one of violence." He regularly published writers of like mind, including a clergyman named Hugh O. Pentecost. Thompson often crossed swords with that paragon of Victorian morality, Goldwin Smith, on the subject of religion's social role. Smith was of the view that "religion was the cement of social order." Pentecost's religious calling gave him the credibility needed to counter such attitudes and Thompson eagerly published his lucid rebuttals. This one is typical: "Nearer and nearer comes the day when the present popular idols will be smashed, when God will have better ones, when the State will give place to society without rules. and without slaves, when guns shall be beaten into table knives and swords into paper cutters, and when policemen's clubs shall be whittled into jackstraws."

Pentecost's ideology appealed to Thompson's sense of the coming revolution. It expressed a healthy hint of anarchism and displayed early signs of the social gospel, which labour would embrace later in the decade. It also suggested that the church had abdicated its responsibility by failing to sympathize with the poor or assist the labour movement in fighting poverty. The church often found itself harshly criticized in the *Advocate*, but Thompson was no atheist. He had been brought up a Quaker but had developed an enthusiasm for theosophy, an unorthodox religion which combined some of the tenets of Buddhism with a belief in universal brotherhood. These traits made it popular among Bellamyite socialists like Thompson who were greatly attracted to Annie Besant, theosophy's most charismatic proponent of the period. Theosophy also advised slow methodical change, which seems to contradict Thompson's call for rapid change through revolution. But that tenet only strengthened his belief in socialism as a life-long commitment requiring great patience as working people slowly became educated in the need for a drastic change in political direction.

If Thompson had given up on the established church, he still saw some hope for achieving reform through electoral politics. He strongly promoted the notion of direct legislation (referenda and plebiscites) and independent political parties. He supported labour candidates in local elections and even ran unsuccessfullly in provincial by-elections in Toronto in 1892 and 1893.

Through it all, the *Advocate* was Thompson's soap box for proclaiming solutions to all the social problems. But more than that, it was his refuge from the "reptile press" or the "prostitute press" where he earned his living. Clearly, Thompson hoped that what started out "purely as a business enterprise" would take off, unshackling him from the mainstream press and allowing him more time to pursue his political interests. When it did not, he sometimes turned on the very people he was attempting to serve.

"The capitalist press denounces Labour Reform and singles out its active leaders for virulent, spiteful abuse," he wrote. "Does he [the workingman] stand by the man under fire and write to the editor telling him what a despicable intellectual prostitute he is? Does he then and there quit taking the paper? Oh, dear no! He never kicks at anything he reads in a paper, unless it happens to be a labour paper and then doesn't he raise an everlasting racket if anything appears that he does not altogether agree with."

The item had a bitter tone uncharacteristic of the man who once wrote humorous political satire as Jimuel Briggs. But Thompson's anger was understandable. With the Knights dying and his dream of an independent labour journal about to turn into a nightmare "because it does not pay expenses," he was a spiritually wounded man.

When the *Advocate* ceased publication on October 2, 1891, it had only a few hundred readers. The popular *Advocate* columnist Ben said the church and the "indifference of the labour men" had "crushed the paper." Thompson was even more irate: "It is much to be regretted that the wage-earners are so stupidly blind to their own interests that they cannot see the advantage of having a live outspoken journal to plead their cause."

Other observers took a contrary view. "If labouring people derive their notions of things, social and political, from the labour journals received by us it is not much to be wondered at if envy and malice and all uncharitableness should be found smouldering in the breasts of the labourers." That's how *Trinity University Review* editor J.G. Carter Troop summarized the role of the labour press in Toronto during the early 1890s. In large part he was referring to the *Advocate*.

With the benefit of hindsight, some historians have argued that the *Advocate*'s failure was as much due to Thompson's individual style and political expression as to the absence of labour support. Historian Wayne Lennon suggests, for example, that Thompson's views were "probably not acceptable to most of his readers and this may help explain the short life of the *Advocate*."

In a cooler moment, Thompson wrote this sober epitaph for his own paper: "If the *Labour Advocate* has done something to prepare the more receptive minds among its readers for this inevitable change, and to show that in socialism alone can be found the solution of the problem, our existence will not have been in vain."

For Thompson, the attractive and tightly edited weekly was another milestone in a career that would continue to influence the labour movement and its press until his death at 90 years of age on May 20, 1933. After the paper folded, he joined Joseph C. McMillan of the *Ontario Workman* and cartoonist John Wilson Bengough at the Grip Printing and Publishing Company, the firm that had printed the *Advocate*. The three helped produce the most popular satirical weekly of the day, *Grip*, appropriately named after a raven in Charles Dickens's novel *Barnaby Rudge*.

Thompson continued to cultivate his socialist views after the death of the *Advocate*, both through his writings and by his active involvement in various groups. In 1892, for example, the Knights published his *Labour Reform Songster*. His byline turned up in Bellamy's *New Nation*. He was active in the Toronto Single Tax Association and Nationalism Association, serving as president of the latter in 1893-94. He also became the first president of the Canadian Socialist League in 1899 and secretary of the Ontario Socialist League in 1902.

In that same year, the Knights were expelled from the Trades and Labour Congress at the Berlin (now Kitchener) convention. During the 1890s, they had made inroads in Quebec but were on the wane in much of the rest of Canada. Through the decade, the order had been assailed with charges of dual unionism or organizing in the same workplace as the union chartered by the TLC. The order had left a strong legacy of the need to organize all workers into unions by industry, but their influence was clearly at an end.

Thompson carried on the fight while supporting himself as a writer of annual reports and the like for several provincial government agencies, including the bureau of mines, the colonization and forestry department and the bureau of industries. He became the Toronto correspondent for the *Labour Gazette*, a new monthly founded in 1900 by the federal labour department under future Liberal prime minister Mackenzie King. He also wrote for mining and textile trade journals and continued to contribute to the labour press, although gradual blindness hindered his output in later years. His efforts to get elected to the Toronto board of education were as fruitless as his early attempts to gain a seat in the legislature. In 1905, for example, he was beaten out by another labour advocate and fellow socialist James Simpson, who later edited the *Industrial Banner*.

As for the *Advocate*, the last of the Knights' impressive fleet of journals, it opened the floodgates for a socialist debate which would preoccupy labour editors for decades to come. It had profoundly influenced labour reform thinking in the early 1890s and set a new high standard for labour journalism. One man who watched in awe and learned much from the *Advocate* was Thompson's contemporary, David Taylor, the editor of a popular Montreal labour paper called the *Echo*.

7

A Labour Advocate for Quebec

As Phillips Thompson was preparing to launch his *Labour Advocate* in Toronto in the fall of 1890, another strong-willed labour editor had already pulled his first few editions from the presses of a Montreal printing shop. David Taylor had taken the editorial helm of the *Echo* that spring when Local 176 of the Montreal Typographical Union struck the *Herald*. The strike paper published until June, then came out with a special edition in September on the as-yet-unproclaimed Labour Day. By early October, Taylor had decided to publish the *Echo* as a weekly "journal for the progressive workman." To broaden its appeal, he published on Saturdays and added what was necessary to make it a "family newspaper" as well.

The eight-page tabloid cost three cents and was quickly endorsed by the Central Trades and Labour Council of Montreal and later by the Dominion Trades and Labour Congress. Although not an official Knights of Labour paper, the *Echo* carried many of the torches held high by Knights journals of the previous decade. Women workers, child labour, shorter hours, the single tax, labour representation—all these issues found column space in the sharply edited Montreal paper.

It wasn't the first time that the largely French-speaking city had seen a labour paper. The *Northern Journal* had published there in the early 1870s as the official organ of the Canadian Labour Protective and Mutual Improvement Association. In 1888 Arthur W. Short had started a short-lived Knights paper called the *Canadian Workman*. French-language labour journals had appeared long before the *Echo* came on the scene. There was *Le Peuple Travailleur* publishing back in the 1850s, for example, and a string of other papers in the 1880s—*L'Artisan* and *L'Ouvrier* in Quebec City, *Le Travailleur Illustré*, *Le Trait d'Union* and the Knights *L'Union Ouvrière* in Montreal. Quebec

City Knights had begun publishing *Le Travail* by 1890, and in nearby Lévis the movement was served by *Le Travailleur de Lévis.*

Like other labour papers, the *Echo* promised to "advocate all measures having for their object the advancement and elevation of the working classes." But it offered a shift in editorial emphasis from that of its predecessors. As the so-called golden era of the Gay Nineties picked up steam, working families began to doubt whether they were meant to share any part of the gold or the gaiety. As reported in the 1889 Royal Commission on the Relations of Labour and Capital—the eighth commission on labour-related issues since 1880—there were some minor improvements in industrial life. But as Taylor observed, the old social problems persisted; the old solutions had failed.

The 1889 report said sanitary conditions in the factories and workers' homes were in an "advanced state." But labour editors knew that things had not advanced much for workers. Their wages remained low and working conditions were still unhealthy and dangerous, despite the commission's view that it had secured "better protection from accident." The report thanked the labour movement, and indirectly its editors, for their "persistent efforts" to bring about an end to child labour, boost educational standards, improve benefits and extend relief to the poor. But as the dawn broke on the new decade, the battle had hardly begun.

Men and women from the farms were moving into the cities to find work in the factories, causing urban centres to bulge at the seams. Clashes resulted as agrarian workers mixed with skilled industrial labour. The government-assisted immigration program added to the overcrowding and caused consternation among workers who saw their jobs being given away to Chinese immigrants.

In Toronto, for example, social historian S.D. Clark described living conditions among poor families. "There is a lack of proper sanitary conditions," he observed, noting that in a local slum there was "one out-door closet [bathroom] for dozens of men, women and children. It is simply disgraceful. Then looking out you can see the garbage piled up as high as the window. Nauseating odors and sights on every hand." He posed the question labour journalists had been asking for two decades or more: "How can children grow up decently in homes like these!"

The situation was no better in Montreal. Using local death rates as a test of how bad things really were, a social activist named Herbert Ames revealed the squalid conditions of life for Montreal's working families. The death rate was a measure of deficiencies in homes and Ames was not surprised to find that the rate in Montreal's working-class slums was almost double what it was in well-to-do neighbourhoods. "In more than half the cases the victims are little children," he wrote in *The City Below the Hill*.

Like American muckrakers of this period—Lincoln Steffens, Ray Stannard Baker, Upton Sinclair, Ida Tarbell—Ames fuelled the flames of social reform by exposing the evils of industry and the inaction, and sometimes corruption, of government and corporations. His shocking accounts of what life was like for the industrial classes inspired the *Echo* editor as he immersed his paper in the debate about socialism as the solution to the horrors documented by Ames and others.

The persistence of social inequality, the continuing exploitation of workers and the oppressive living conditions of working families led most labour reformers to embrace one socialist doctrine or another in the 1890s. Though some historians suggest that socialism held little appeal for Canadian labour, Taylor, like Thompson, whom he greatly admired and called "a sterling labour reformer," loaded the *Echo* with talk of the new socialist dawn. Socialist theories, independent socialist labour parties and even the social role of the church filled the pages of the *Echo*.

While the lines between the labour movement and industrial capitalists were being drawn, behind the scenes labour was slowly moving into position for a kind of civil war between reformers and radicals. The *Echo* reflected the coming storm with its coverage of the socialist debates in Europe and America. Though he devoted less and less editorial space to them, Taylor also continued to call for support of the old social panaceas—co-operation, opposition to government-assisted Chinese immigration and even temperance. "No man can rightly call himself a labour reformer who is not in favour of restricting or abolishing the liquor traffic," wrote the "Our Boarding House" columnist.

Taylor saw clearly that the movement had to shift away from any notion of a cosy worker-owner alliance such as labour advocates had dreamed of during an earlier period of Canada's economic development. He helped set the stage for the labour movement's final exit from the old producer ideology of Isaac Buchanan back in the days of the *Workingman's Journal* and into the new industrial capitalist era.

With that same clarity, Taylor intended to expose the social inadequacies of the new system. "The publishers of the *Echo* belong to the class to whom they especially appeal for support— the workingmen," Taylor wrote in his opening editorial. "Knowing many wrongs under which our working population suffers, we shall be able to hold them up to public view and demand their redress, nor rest satisfied till this is accomplished."

Inviting correspondence on all social and political questions, the *Echo* editor ensured that readers would have something to comment on by publishing provocative opinions in columns like "The Social Problem" and "Our Boarding House." Reminiscent of the earlier writings of Enjolras in the *Palladium of Labour*, these were imaginative ways of bringing workers up to date on the latest views of labour luminaries. Cyrille Horsiot, one such contributor, fast became the weekly's resident social philosopher.

A committed socialist, Horsiot generated pages of copy for Taylor on the "morality of the capitalistic system of industry," as one headline put it. Like Thompson and others, he also wrote songs and poetry for the worker, some of which inevitably found its way into the *Echo*. But regardless of the form his writing took and regardless of the subject, Horsiot relentlessly attacked capitalism as the chief enemy of the working class. On health and safety, for example, he penned some of the most moving passages of any labour journalist.

"It is frightful to see the death of scores of men on duty in the mines, railways, buildings, at sea, and everywhere," he wrote, "some entombed full of life, others crushed to jelly or scalded, while others are drowned like rats in a pit or burned alive as the Saracens of Spain were in the good old time. But it is more frightful to be a witness of the moral death, when the body so odiously continues to walk, to lead, and to move its mechanical existence, while there is already no more spirit, no manhood in this useless being." Horsiot closed with this eloquent piece of rhetoric: "How many deaths are occuring day by day caused by the saw mill of the human spirit, bones and flesh, which is called capitalism?"

In somewhat less inspired style, the "Our Boarding House" columnist argued that it "is time that these corporations [i.e., railways] are taught that human lives are of greater importance than the dollars and cents; it is time that they are taught that citizens have rights which they must respect."

The *Echo* proudly offered health care advice to the working family. Seldom did an edition appear without its two pages of advertisements crammed with cures for everything from smoking and an overworked brain to cancer. In one of them, hard-working students were encouraged to avoid "unstrung nerves, insomnia, dispepsia or indigestion" by taking "Paine's Celery Compound." It was the type of ad that labour press readers had become used to over the years amidst others for cigars, hardware and items from the haberdashery.

Another social issue that raised Taylor's ire was the lack of provision for elderly workers. One article spoke of an old couple, a man, 70, and a woman, 60, who had "committed suicide together because they were to be turned out of house and home for non-payment of rent." On the related matter of housing, Taylor called for a "general clearing out of the unsanitary dens which infest the eastern and central portions of the city, and the erection in their stead of tenement houses of moderate rental constructed on modern sanitary principles."

Child labour was a third major concern for Taylor, and he gave Horsiot whatever space he requested to expose the practice. "In factories, where labour-saving machinery has reached its most perfect and wonderful development," the *Echo*'s Enjolras wrote, "little children [are] debarred from their legitimate and only inheritance—the school." In a single sentence, Horsiot managed to hint at the evils of technological change and raise the question of compulsory education, both popular topics in the labour press.

Also popular, as we have seen, was the stand taken against Chinese immigrants. Racist remarks were an unseemly trademark of labour journals, but Taylor's socialist analysis helped him put the question into a larger perspective. The workers, he suggested, realize that "capitalism is continually encroaching upon this right [to life] and that the importation of Chinese and cheap pauper labour is but another move on the part of capital to make labour more dependent and submissive."

Oddly enough, Taylor's long list of causes virtually excluded the issue of equality for women workers. Unlike the Knights papers, there was no mention of women in the masthead. Often the *Echo* seemed to take a negative approach, seeing women workers as another group, like the Chinese, who were simply displacing male workers. Indeed, the view that women were standing in the way of men's advancement got prominent coverage. "Considering the place woman occupies in the world," one contributor wrote, "having to watch and guide the early footsteps of man, and teach him during his tender years, his duties in life and, in fact, help very materially in forming his character, and prepare him for the coming struggle—I would suggest, in view of these facts, that, as a national and social measure, female labour in the workshop be abolished by Act of parliament." The writer eloquently concluded: "Let man be monarch in the field of labour, and reverenced in his house, and let woman do her share of life's duties apportioned to her by Providence."

That hard-line commentary brought more than a few letters to the editor and the loud clamour may have persuaded Taylor that he should come to the defence of women, especially when they were fighting for the right to organize and for equal pay for equal work. Countering the sting of the above writer, another commentator noted that "women are the greatest sufferers from low wages. The cruelest feature of the wage situation is that women standing side by side with men in the same shops and stores are paid far less wages for the same work. This is an aristocracy of sex that shames and belies all of our claims to democracy."

Taylor was well aware of the issues affecting women workers but he often missed the boat. Still, he partly redeemed himself by running items on women's experiences on the job. Already in the 1890s, Montreal was becoming a sweatshop for seamstresses. Taylor showed the underbelly of such workplaces by running this almost poetic description of the life of a female factory worker. "She worked all day in the cloak factory. Stitch, stitch, stitch, all day, until her eyes smarted and her fingers were weary. Every day and every day just the same, and only $4 a week. At night she went home to a small, poor room, to a frugal supper, to her lonely thoughts and her hard-earned slumbers."

If the *Echo* toyed with the old social solutions, it also proposed some challenging new ones. Profit-sharing, for example, received much comment in the *Echo*. Land nationalization, the single tax and anti-monopoly which had often been proposed in labour papers, now took on new urgency. "With the establishment of a single tax," one writer suggested, "land monopoly would disappear, and the power of the few to levy blackmail on the many would be destroyed."

The need to organize unions was becoming more intense as an unfettered capitalist economy explored new ways to exploit workers. The role of the church occupied more space in the *Echo*, a sign that welfare and charity, once the exclusive domain of organized religion, could be shared with organized labour. Still, a coalition of the two into a powerful social force was hardly right around the corner. "The reason the workingman does not attend church," one writer argued, "is that the capitalist, as a rule, is a man who goes to church; and the relations between them and their employees are not so cordial during the six days of the week as to make the workman wish to be anywhere near them on the seventh."

For the more radical labour and social reformers, all of these solutions combined would still fall far short without gaining political power, socialist in nature. Taylor believed that vital public protections through social insurance, an end to patronage, the abolition of the Senate, and equality for all would come only through socialism. But the worker had to be wary of calls for violent revolution. As usual, Horsiot epitomized the *Echo* editor's sentiments. "When violent attempts at revolution fail, greater despotism results," he lectured. "If the wage-slave succeeds not in breaking his fetters, he draws the halter tighter round his neck. An appeal to the bullet in a country where the ballot can be used as effectively, if used intelligently, is an acknowledgement on the part of revolutionists that they are in a hopeless minority, for when workingmen are too stupid or too ignorant to vote for their rights instead of parties, they are certainly too cowardly to fight for them."

Again, the "Our Boarding House" writer put it less eloquently but more succinctly. "Female labour, pauper and contract labour, shorter hours, lien and factory acts, land and money reform, and all the thousand and one things demanded won't settle it unless you legislate rent, profit, and interest out of existence, by forming a gigantic combine of the people, by the people, and for the people."

It was a battle cry heard round the labour movement, but the *Echo* was not to be its champion for long. Like Thompson's

Labour Advocate, Taylor's paper failed in the fall of 1891, leaving trade unionists temporarily without a voice. As late as 1893 at a Dominion Trades and Labour Congress executive meeting, according to historian Eugene Forsey, the president "deplored the disappearance of the Montreal *Echo*, because of lack of interest."

After a brief lull, Taylor replenished his energies and in May 1894, *Saturday Times*, his new "Journal of Current Thought and Opinion" began circulating in the streets of Montreal. Much respected by labour reformers, it was one of the most progressive alternative weeklies of its day. But it too failed in November 1895, causing the *People's Voice*, a Winnipeg labour paper of which we shall read more, to blast organized labour in eastern Canada. "Accept outside advice; get together on one common ground, sink personal feelings and petty jealousies, and resurrect that excellent paper—*Saturday Times*," the Prairie weekly advised.

Whether the Quebec labour movement ever accepted the advice is not known. However, it seems that Montreal's labour advocates did not find as effective a voice as Taylor's papers until several years later. In fact, the movement would not be so well served again until a paper called *Cotton's Weekly* in Cowansville, Quebec, took centre stage as the new voice of the socialist labour movement in 1908. Meanwhile, in southern Ontario, the socialist crusade was continuing through the efforts of another new labour paper, the *Industrial Banner*, in London.

8

For the Weak Against the Strong

Joseph T. Marks was not a founding member of the Knights of Labour, but he became one of the order's most tireless organizers. A sheet metal worker with the Grand Trunk Railway in his home town of London, Ontario, he visited local assemblies and signed up new members as he travelled through southern Ontario, lecturing workers on the merits of trade unionism. In the late 1880s, "Joe" Marks became general secretary of Knights Local Assembly 7110, where he worked vigorously to stimulate a revival of the near moribund Knights movement.

By the spring of 1890, he was "Master Workman" of District Assembly 138 and he redoubled his efforts to keep the Knights alive, meeting with members, travelling at his own expense, at times carrying on even while sick. When it appeared that the order was virtually dead, Marks attempted to resurrect the principles of the Knights by founding the Industrial Brotherhood of Canada, an organization set up to "develop the intelligence of individual workers." The energetic tinsmith was also involved in the founding of an educational experiment called the Open Forum, later the Radical Club. He may also have learned some of his publishing skills while working on the *Searchlight*, the organ of the Canadian Co-operative Commonwealth. It was all excellent preparation for his future role as editor of the *Industrial Banner*.

Marks and other London unionists founded a volunteer organization called the Labour Educational Association to publish the *Banner* and he would remain its secretary-treasurer until his death. He and H.B. Ashplant, Frank Plant and Rudolph Russell, started the paper in the spring of 1891 and its leaflet size probably made it the smallest labour paper ever published in the country. It was soon enlarged, however, and from the outset Marks ensured that it would have an influence on labour affairs disproportionate to its physical size. "For the right against the wrong! For the weak against the strong!" was the slogan under the *Banner* flag. And Marks promised the London Trades and Labour Council, which had endorsed the four-page paper, that he would do his best to make the lively tabloid worth every penny of its five-cent cover price.

Under Marks's editorship the *Banner* quickly became the clarion of the London labour movement. Claiming no interest in profit, the young labour advocate told readers that the paper would be "the foremost exponent of social and municipal reforms" and that it would act as "an educator of public opinion on economic and social questions."

Like Phillips Thompson, Marks was single-minded about the ultimate solution to society's problems. "Co-operation, pure and simple, is the coming system," he predicted. "Call it collectivism, nationalism, socialism, or what you will, it all means the same thing." Always ready to back words with action, Marks soon set about founding another organization, the Forward Movement. The purpose of it was "to band the wage earners of this country into an organization that will make them practically independent of the capitalists." Marks used his paper to urge membership in the new movement.

With the *Banner* he intended to champion the cause of the poor and the unemployed, speaking out on issues of the day affecting all groups of citizens suffering under the industrial system. With only a single page of advertisements, there was plenty of room for the exposure of social ills and the discussion of labour's solutions.

One of the perceived social ills was Chinese immigration, and like his predecessors, Marks took out labour's frustrations with the government's immigration policy on the Chinese workers. Considering himself somewhat of an expert on the question, he described the oriental immigrants' work and social habits as loathsome. The *Banner* editor urged readers to "agitate this question everywhere until the government shall be compelled to act and stem the tide of undesirable Mongolian immigration."

Monopoly, that old enemy of labour from back in the days when the *Palladium* was in its prime, was another omnipresent evil. Convinced that all "natural monopolies," such as railways, should be nationalized, the *Banner* editor struck a blow against them whenever possible. He reprinted the following item from J.A. Wayland's famed "free-lance socialistic periodical," the *Appeal to Reason,* showing the evil at work on the elderly. "Robbed of his earnings through monopoly, as fast as he created it, his life one continual drudge," noted the Girard, Kansas, paper, the elderly worker is left "with nothing but the poor house or private charity as a reward."

Inadequate housing and poverty in general were other social problems that Marks used to illustrate the inhumanity of the system. "Rent, interest and profit are only secondary names for robbery, theft and plunder," he suggested, giving more column space to these questions than to most other social issues.

Not a journalist or printer by trade, Marks often relied on reprints from other papers, but in this item on worker exploitation he clearly needed no outside help: "The deserving poor are but the natural products of a vicious social system that puts a premium on rascality and idleness by defrauding and degrading the labourer whose enterprise and energy are unfairly manipulated to keep in luxury and affluence a class of idlers whose chief aim would seem to be the oppression of their fellow men."

He meant fellow women as well, of course, for he saw female workers as one of the groups that suffered most under the burgeoning industrial system. Although the *Banner* did not cover the issue as regularly as some earlier labour papers, Marks usually gave it some prominence. In one front-page item he called it "scandalous" that "working girls" were forced to labour under the harshest of conditions and insisted on stricter enforcement of the Factories Act.

The *Banner* was no less concerned about child labour, still an all-too-common practice in the 1890s. Although Marks and his wife Emily do not appear to have had children of their own, he still shouted "No" to their exploitation with the passion of a parent. "It is not well with the child. Nor can it always be prosperous for those who disport in luxury upon the ill-paid labour of little hands."

To these symptoms of general social malaise, Marks proposed the same cures traditionally advocated by the labour movement. He embraced the quest for an eight-hour day with great interest, giving a new twist to the old arguments. "Why should men work even eight hours a day," he asked, "when the advanced mechanical skill and productive power of the world is sufficient to feed, clothe, house and provide every luxury requisite to happiness with less than four hours of toil a day?"

Marks was also a great supporter of the single tax. Like others, he believed it would end land speculation. He wanted to ensure that land use was "the rightful title of occupancy." Then the value of the land "caused by the congregation of population and the erection of homes, schools, churches and manufactories will be shared by the people whose enterprise created it."

Marks often turned from his own prophesying to criticism of the church for its failure to shield the workers from social injustice. "Workingmen are not drifting from the church," he observed, "but the church is drifting from the workingmen, when she refuses to denounce injustice in high places, and remains silent on those great questions that vitally affect humanity."

Government, too, was an abysmal failure at curing the economic and social maladies that plagued workers and their families. Marks called for a "proper electoral system such as proportional representation." He hailed the use of referenda to make public decisions and supported labour candidates wherever they appeared on the ballot. With a single tax on landlords as the general form of taxation, fair political representation and nationalized monopolies, "it would not be long before the people . . . would gradually evolve a co-operative system of industry that would assuredly kill the present system of competition."

Unquestionably a socialist, Marks would later call for "a most radical and far-reaching change of base," a veiled cry for revolution that was typical of his style. "Individualism," he later wrote, "has turned many people into thieves and scoundrels because of a system of competition which presses honest people to the wall."

By the mid-1890s, the paper had made yet another format change—there would be four in all—and plans were being laid to expand. Soon Hamilton and Toronto were also served by the *Banner*. The weekly changed to a monthly as Marks struggled to maintain the relatively high quality of the paper while expanding coverage to include the new labour communities. Often he would work for nothing, only drawing an occasional $10 stipend.

Marks was ahead of his time in his method of distributing the paper. To this day, many union publications do not arrive by mail at the members' doorsteps. The *Banner* was mailed directly to the homes of members of subscribing unions at 20 cents a year. Of course, any labour body could get bulk copies of the paper at cost and many jumped at the chance. The subsequent over-runs thrilled the London Advertiser Printing Company, which had been founded by *Globe* editor James Cameron, a Knights sympathizer. The extra orders sometimes pushed the *Banner*'s regular press run of 2,500 up to as high as 15,000 at the exhorbitant cost of $226!

The *Banner* was becoming so popular that the local public librarian, a Mr. Blackwell, felt compelled, probably with coaxing from Marks, to comment on the fact in an article entitled "Is the *Banner* Read?" "In our last issue we recommended to the public that they read Ignatius Donnelly's book 'Caesar's Column'. . . . Since the recommendation in the *Banner*, Librarian Blackwell says there has been a constant demand for the work." It was not exactly a scientific readership survey, but it nevertheless led Marks to conclude that "there is no doubt but what the *Banner* is read, and well read, too."

Despite his notable success, Marks's editorship was not without its problems. At one point, friction developed when some members of the London Trades and Labour Council became suspicious of Marks's motives. Tempers had been frayed through internal arguments and the general frustration caused by a street railway strike in downtown London. Although no one accused Marks of any specific wrongdoing, there was the suggestion that no man would give so freely of his time and money as Marks did. There was even the hint of questionable "financial transactions in regard to the *Industrial Banner*."

Marks publicly rebuffed the charge by requesting that an investigative committee be appointed to report on the said transactions. The council leaders stressed that they had confidence in the editor, but he insisted on the investigation and on a public announcement of its findings. Marks told the committee that he could prove he had spent over $500 of his own money in supporting the street railway strike, and that didn't include lost time.

The committee ordeal added pressure to Marks's already gruelling schedule and might have seriously threatened the *Banner*'s existence, but Marks was ever steady. Not every labour editor would have been up to it. Philip Obermeyer, of the Hamilton Trades and Labour Council, made a strong case for quitting the thankless task in a report on the impending closure of the *Banner*'s Hamilton edition. "I positively retire from connection with it at tonight's meeting," the discouraged editor wrote, "as I have not had the slightest help from any of the members, and cannot give up any more of my time."

The longevity of Marks's editorship is all the more remarkable considering the predictably short lives of so many of the *Banner*'s contemporaries. As we have seen, Toronto's *Advocate* and Montreal's *Echo* died bitter and untimely deaths the year the *Banner* began publishing. Many other labour journals around the country also suffered quick and painful deaths in the early 1890s.

The *Signal and Workman's Advocate* in Truro, Nova Scotia, began publishing in August 1890, but doesn't appear to have lived out the year. Another Maritime paper, the *Workman*, started in September 1892, when Local 85 of the International Typographical Union struck the Saint John *Progress* in New Brunswick. It probably lasted only a year or two, for the local was again struggling to found a labour paper, the *Weekly Toiler*, in 1895. As testament to the difficulty of starting such papers, the east coast labour movement didn't get another voice until printers in Halifax started a strike paper called the *Weekly News* in 1899.

With only the *Banner* to serve Toronto area workers, labour advocates supported the founding of an eight-page tabloid called the *Worker* in June 1894. Several other papers reprinted from it and it won the praise of other labour editors, but it too soon faded. In Ottawa, there were no less than four attempts to nurture a local labour press between 1893 and 1896. The *Wage-Earner* published briefly, then probably succumbed to the *Free Lance*, which began in October 1893.

The *Free Lance* was a weekly for all seasons. Trying to cover as large a readership as possible, it "Published in the Interests of Labour, Temperance, Single Tax, Municipal, Provincial, Federal Reform, Societies, Home Circle, and General News." But it didn't have an open field for long. In May 1894, *Capital Siftings* came on the scene to challenge the *Free Lance*'s claim to labour journal status.

Siftings editor J.G. Kilt openly defied the *Free Lance*'s supremacy by charging two cents instead of three, but he failed to get an endorsement from the local labour council. For a time the Ottawa labour community benefitted from the competition. Unfortunately, like the earlier battles in Toronto among Knights editors, the rivalry turned nasty. In July 1894, Kilt angrily attacked "J.W.P.," the *Free Lance* editor, saying that he "should be hung about his desk until eventually he uses it as an epitaph for his insignificant little paper, which is a disgrace to labour." Two years later, after much name-calling in the pages of both papers, the *Free Lance* became the more commercial Ottawa *Tribune*.

Out on the west coast, George F. Leaper had started one of the earliest British Columbia labour weeklies in February 1893. The *People's Journal* was a "co-operative labour paper," according to historian Eugene Forsey. But it lasted only about three months. Again, it illustrated the incredible energy and dedication required to edit a 19th-century labour journal.

Marks remained at the helm of the *Banner* for 28 years, always stressing the pragmatic solution in his quest to aid the workers. More inclined to set up co-operatives than to simply editorialize about them, he gained the wide respect of other labour advocates, including James Simpson, who would later help start the Toronto edition of the *Banner*.

Born in Lancashire, England, Simpson had come to Canada with his family in 1888 at 14 years of age. Like Marks, he started out working in a tin factory, but soon moved to the composing room of the *Toronto Evening News*. A printers' strike took the young apprentice to the *Evening Star*, a strike paper which printed several weekly reform papers, for a time including Goldwin's Smith's *Weekly Sun* and George Wrigley's *Citizen and Country*.

Simpson eventually became a reporter and then municipal editor at the *Star*, but his reading of the Wrigley paper helped convert him to socialism and make him an ardent labour advocate. In 1903, he was elected president of the Toronto Trades and Labour Council, which at the time had about 10,000 members. But his tenure was short-lived, for a group of anti-socialist council members worked to oust him in an election six months later. In 1904, Simpson, a strong Methodist, helped found the Toronto Labour Temple. In 1908, he ran for mayor on a socialist ticket and eventually won a seat on the board of control.

In the spring of 1912, Simpson, Marks and others met in the Toronto Labour Temple to discuss founding a provincial *Banner*. The result was the formation of the Labour Educational Publishing Company, an offshoot of the Labour Educational Association which had become a province-wide body. The company incorporated the London-based *Banner* and made its headquarters in Toronto. That October, the first weekly edition of the new paper appeared, with Marks continuing as its editor. The event was celebrated by a huge demonstration at which Simpson outlined the goals of the new paper. He was followed at the speaker's podium by prominent British socialist James Keir Hardie, who called on the paper to help unite the working-class movement.

In the first issue, enlarged to eight pages and with an impressive press run of 25,000, Simpson noted that the *Banner* was "for the education of men and women engaged and interested in the labour movement and to promote the best interests of that movement industrially and politically." The paper continued publishing through the First World War, against which it conducted a vigorous campaign. According to Marks, Simpson deserved the lion's share of the credit for keeping the paper alive.

After Marks's death, Simpson and Tom Stephenson continued to publish the *Banner* until February 24, 1922, but the paper never achieved the same status it had held under Marks. His dedication to the paper and the labour movement were held in high regard by labour editors everywhere. Arthur Puttee, the editor of the Winnipeg *Voice*, was one of Marks's greatest admirers. Calling the tinsmith-turned-labour-advocate an "everlasting stayer," he tried to emulate his practical ways. The effort seems to have paid off, for the *Voice* published well into the 20th century.

9

A Western Voice Speaks Out

Sitting down at his printer's bench, C.C. Steuart composed a house advertisement addressed to Winnipeg businesses for insertion in the *People's Voice*. "The *Voice* starts today with a guaranteed circulation of 1,000 copies," claimed the youthful, almost baby-faced Steuart. "Not bad for a new paper, eh?" he added in his cocky style. He was nearing the launch date of June 16, 1894, so the *Voice* editor hurried to get the eight-page tabloid ready for his Saturday morning readers.

Steuart, a printer who had moved to Manitoba from Ontario, was soon boasting that the new weekly was the "only labour paper published in Western Canada," and that its circulation would jump to 1,500 by the end of its first month. He was probably correct on both counts, but other papers had made the same predictions, and had gone the way of the dinosaur soon enough. In the 1880s, no fewer than four labour journals had attempted to cover the vast territory west of the Ontario border. Winnipeg had been a centre of Knights of Labour activity and they had published the *Call* and the *Industrial News*. Calgary, Vancouver and Victoria had also broken ground with their own journals. None of them had seen their circulation promises fulfilled. The *Voice*, however, would be different.

By August 1894, after only two months, Steuart and his two business partners, O. Anderson and O. Partington, claimed a press run of 4,000. Local merchants were indeed impressed with this new paper "Published in the Interests of the Labouring Classes." They apparently rushed to its 158 Bannatyne Street East offices to buy space at 10 cents a line in hopes of luring the *Voice*'s fast-expanding audience. Steuart's membership in a local retailers' association, formed as a pressure group for early shop closings, also may have helped the likeable editor attract ads. In any event, western Canada's "pioneer labour paper" was soon forced to increase its ad columns and then eventually to expand the whole paper to accommodate "the demand upon our advertising space."

It was an auspicious start, and one that must be credited to Steuart's tireless efforts to sell the paper as an "outspoken independent journal in the labour and general reform movement." The *Voice* was quickly endorsed and supported by the Winnipeg Trades and Labour Council and Steuart aimed to please local labour advocates. The paper would be "fearless in advocacy of clean federal, provincial and municipal administrations, ever alert to put down 'snobbishness' and better the state of social conditions of this grand western country."

Like earlier labour press successes, few as they were, Steuart made a go of it partly because he brought some light-hearted humour and vitality to his work. Instead of attempting to browbeat workers into subscribing to the paper, for example, Steuart tried his hand at poetry to captivate their interest. The following rhyming couplets were addressed to a worker's spouse:

"Twill cost him but a dollar, which sum would well be spent
In helping on the paper which for workingmen is meant,
For where he'd learn by reading of what is taking place
Within the world of labour, in improving this great race
Of Labouring humanity—their struggles, triumphs, blows
Are pictured in these columns—by Steuart C's bellows."

It was no worse than much of the doggerel that passed for working-class poetry and literature in the 19th century, and it seemed to bring results. On a more serious note, Steuart supplied potential readers with plenty of other reasons to subscribe. "Newspapers run by capitalists and syndicates will only give a half-hearted support to that section of industry which most requires support," he wrote. "The only way to have an independent press is to establish it yourselves and be sure that it receives support sufficient to keep it free."

Steuart struck a chord with Winnipeg labour advocates and they hailed the appearance of the new paper. On September 3, 1894, the occasion of Canada's first Labour Day, the local typographers' union put out a commemorative tabloid called the *Winnipeg Typographer*. Steuart, an International Typographical Union member, saw an opportunity to broaden his audience. He placed an ad in the paper claiming to be

"free from political or sectarian influence." He also noted that
the *Voice* would "promote the union principle amongst all workers, of both sexes, and of all shades of opinion."

Here was a forum for the fight for eight hours, temperance, the destruction of monopolies, the nationalization of
land and the creation of a single tax. To help him sustain the
forum, the *Voice* editor found some of the ablest commentators
in Winnipeg, and not all of them were men, as had most often
been the case with previous papers.

A letter signed "Mrs. Unionism," for example, called on
"all right-thinking women, in fact, all women, to help in the
cause of labour." Mrs. Charles Hislop, the wife of a Ward 4
alderman and labour council activist, stated the case for giving
the vote to woman with some dignity. "Woman's suffrage will
elevate the condition of both husband and wife," she wrote.
"Woman demands no special laws; she asks her place as a
citizen and wishes only to stand free, side by side with her
brother man, to aid in working out the highest destiny of
humanity."

The *Voice* wasn't content to leave readers with the idea
that women should only stand behind their union men, either.
In an item entitled "Woman Union Leader," Steuart saluted a
Belleville, Ontario, labour leader. In another he quoted Cora
D. Hind on the issue of pay equity. "As a matter of self-
protection, if for no other motive," she said, "men should cry
aloud for equal pay for equal work without reference to sex."

Voice writers were equally forceful in presenting their views
on child labour. "Take all the children out of the workshop,"
one article bluntly demanded, "and put them in the school."
In one edition, Steuart himself took up the pen on behalf of
children after a starving immigrant boy wandered through the
paper's offices begging for food. "Is it not inexcusable in a
new country to have old-fashioned misery such as this?" he
asked readers. Then he turned the story of the starving boy
into an attack on the church. Children starve in the midst of
plenty, he wrote, and they "grow up ignorant and dangerous
to society, whilst smug preachers persuade comfortable con-
gregations to contribute towards paying off the church mortgage."

It was stuff written out of high passion for the cause and
it attracted more of the same, particularly when the subject
was poverty. A local social reform advocate named John Peter
Paulby was impressed by Steuart's paper and quickly volunteered

to write a regular column. One of his favourite subjects was the Winnipeg slums. Here he describes a part of the city's famed North End called New Jerusalem: "What a frightful state many of the hovels are in! In the first place those buildings would not make a respectable cowshed. In the second, the space for occupation does not exceed two small rooms, and in these whole families live. In the third, the surroundings are of the most dismal kind and cannot but have a tendency to breed disease."

If Paulby was the reporter on the beat, so to speak, then William Small was the *Voice*'s philosopher and chief strategist for encouraging social change. Although not as fine or humorous a writer as Phillips Thompson, Small still brought labour's solutions to the fore with fire and compassion. He worked as a carpenter for the Canadian Pacific Railway and was considered a sterling trade unionist with a history going back to the Knights of Labour at the peak of their power. An active temperance advocate and Presbyterian, he had earned wide respect in the community.

As Winnipeg's elder labour statesman, Small wrote long and detailed tracts on all the social problems facing working families. On the question of housing, for example, he proposed that the city's vacant lands be used to house the poor, workers and their families. He agreed with proposals for building co-operatives, and he pushed for an unemployment insurance scheme. Temperance, the single tax, unionism and socialism were other topics of his regular column.

Unfortunately, Small and several other *Voice* writers saved their most vicious commentaries for the Chinese immigration question. In the west, as elsewhere, the federal government's assisted immigration policy posed a serious threat to jobs that might have gone to non-oriental workers. The *Voice* responded with racist labels of "scourge," "curse" and "undesirable class." Writer Nana Pauline was perhaps the most unkind of all when she discouraged people from using Chinese businesses. "Why not bestow your patronage upon people of your own kind—clean, proper living, live-and-let-live Christian people—whom you would not be ashamed of associating with every day of your lives?" she asked. For Steuart, it was one of the few blotches on the record of his crusading labour paper. More often than not, he followed his own rule of being "outspoken and courageous in the cause of right, willingly espousing the side of the oppressed against the encroachments of those who wield power unjustly."

Socialism gradually began to supplant other solutions that the *Voice* had championed. Even in his comments on public education, Steuart started to see the socialist ideal. "The public school system is socialism," he wrote. "The poor children, whose parents have little property [and therefore] pay hardly any municipal [school] tax, receive the same benefit as the rich man's children." It wasn't as simple as that, but Steuart concluded hopefully that this meant "All men are socialists, though they [may] not know it."

But Steuart's push for socialism was not to reach full maturity in the *Voice*. By May 1897, he was preparing his last editorial, having sold the People's Voice Company to fellow Winnipeg labour advocate Arthur W. Puttee. The latter, along with two fellow typographical union members, Harry Cowan and Gustavus Pingle, had hastily formed the Voice Publishing Company to take over the paper. Clearly a victim of burnout, Steuart sadly handed the office keys to his successor, noting that "as has been the experience of all who have devoted their energy to social reform, we have had a struggle."

Puttee and his partners changed little of Steuart's well-received editorial policy, choosing to emphasize the paper's independence and their intention to "keep away from creeds and denominational fences." They planned to support trade unionism and labour reform and to level the *Voice*'s sites on monopolies. Puttee particularly wanted to use the paper to cheer on government ownership.

For the first year, Cowan took on the lion's share of the editing and managerial duties. Then in May 1898, the paper was beset with a new financial crisis. Cowan left for Vancouver where he became president of the Vancouver Trades and Labour Council and manager of the *Independent*. That left Puttee, who had played a peripheral role the first year, to attend to the rescue operation.

A journeyman printer at the Winnipeg *Free Press*, Puttee was easily capable of replacing Cowan. He quickly set about expanding the profitable job-printing wing of the company to subsidize the *Voice*, since subscriptions, sales and ads did not begin to sustain the weekly. The effort restored the paper's economic vitality, especially with the introduction of a new Thorne typesetting machine.

Puttee was also a man with political ambitions and under his editorship the *Voice* was to become more involved than ever in discussing political solutions to social problems. The *Voice* had always been political. Under Steuart, it had given front-page play to the founding of the Canada Labour Party, for example, which included the usual list of "social demands" in its platform. But Puttee, who had only come to Canada from Britain in 1888, stoked the fire with much comment on the British system of labour representation. Steuart failed to map out a successful business course for the paper, but he had been a strong rhetorical voice for socialism. Now Puttee, who was coy about his views on socialism and never fully embraced it, would be responsible for steering the paper through the hard-bitten socialist debates that marked his early editorship.

"Paulby's Ponderings" continued as before, as did Small's long 'think pieces' on everything from suffrage and the "hireling press" to Senate reform and, of course, socialism. They were joined by others, equally as forceful in making their beliefs known, especially on political questions of the day. Among them were several prominent Americans, including the socialist Eugene V. Debs, future labour historian John R. Commons, and an up-and-coming labour leader named Samuel Gompers, the powerful patriarch of the American Federation of Labour.

A young Canadian, who would earn his spurs in the United States as a union specialist for the wealthy Rockefeller family, also appeared in the *Voice*. His name was William Lyon Mackenzie King, and he would soon list the founding of the federal government's monthly periodical, the *Labour Gazette*, among his other accomplishments. And to keep all eyes glued to the *Voice*, Puttee threw in a story or two from Sir Arthur Conan Doyle's repertoire of Sherlock Holmes escapades.

On the home front, three very able writers joined the list of contributors. While Small busied himself running for the aldermanic seat vacated by Charles Hislop in working-class Ward 4, "W.O.G." took on the church and the economists. "Libertas" dealt with the poverty issue, social conditions and the "social conflict between the classes and the masses." A newcomer named Esau Brammell began writing a front-page column called "Our Social System," in which he revealed that "conditions of society today give rise to the most anarchic inequality and are most iniquitously burdensome to the masses of the people." For Brammell, "co-operation, fraternity, justice, are better principles to found social systems upon than cupidity, greed and grab." Where Brammell left off, an Ontario writer named T.A. Foreman took his place, pushing always for the socialist cause. When Small came second in the city elections, he too returned to his pen.

Puttee saw to it that all the contentious issues got an airing— contract and prison labour, the eight-hour day, education, monopolies. The "effect of Mongolian labour" merited the usual treatment. One item proposed the creation of a union of white laundry workers to combat the Chinese "blight."

A member of Local 191 of the Winnipeg Typographical Union since 1891 and its president in 1893 and 1894, Puttee also made sure there was plenty of news about printers and their unions. Although he had originally come to Portage La Prairie from Folkestone, England, to try his hand at homesteading, he soon returned to the printing business. At first he led the life of an itinerant journeyman in the United States, where he was first inducted into the International Typographical Union at St. Paul, Minnesota. But he longed to be back under British rule. Returning to Canada in 1891, he soon secured a job first with the Brandon *Sun*, then with the *Free Press* in Winnipeg.

The *Voice* editor and his wife shared a rented house on Alfred Avenue with their six children and their large back yard was used as a neighbourhood playground. Puttee's own childhood had been marred by a permanent falling out with his father and the experience had helped fashion him into a crusader for children and improved family life. In one item he was enraged when he learned that a Mrs. Harrison had been "driven crazy" and sent to an insane asylum after her children were forcibly taken from her by the Children's Aid Society.

As an active Unitarian, Puttee had strong views on the need for a religious upbringing, but he seldom let them creep into his editorials. More often, he provided space for sermons by others on social issues viewed from a Christian perspective. When he did discuss the subject, it was usually to defend religious freedom or to attack church tax exemptions as a narrowing of the necessary separation of church and state.

On the lighter side, he inserted the occasional sports item, a "Children's Column," poem or anecdote. One item praised cocaine, "this wonderful drug," as an excellent pain killer!

The mix was so successful that at one point, Puttee immod-
estly called the *Voice* the "best paper of its class in the Dominion."

Under Puttee, the paper both lauded and chided women
workers. He was married to a Folkestone grocer's daughter
named Gertrude M. Strood in 1892 and seems to have held the
view that a woman's best role was in support of her union
husband. Even so, Mrs. Puttee was active in the political community, helping to organize the Women's Labour League which
advocated unions for women. She also turned her house into
an informal social agency which offered a bed to mothers whose
sick children were visiting a city hospital.

There was no doubting the paper's good intentions to
bolster the efforts of women workers to unionize. For example, Winnipeg's first women's union at the Emerson and Hague
overall factory must have derived much courage from the paper's
sympathetic coverage of its early struggle for recognition. Despite
a patronizing tone, articles like the one entitled "For a Living
Wage—Business Crushes the Defenceless Women Workers" must
have been tremendous morale boosters to the 50 striking workers. "A woman has a just right to labour for her own support,"
the item concluded.

But Puttee could also destroy all the good he had done
with such coverage. When it came to the rights of women
workers at the expense of jobs for men, he supported the
latter. He saw no contradiction, for example, in publishing an
article by the Rev. S.G. Smith in which he states that "The
world would be better off if all women were turned out of
their jobs."

Coverage of child labour and the education question were
also regular topics in the *Voice*. Puttee, whose own formal
education ended at age 14, saw the lack of schooling as the
"greatest obstacle in the way of labour reforms." Without it,
the masses could "not grasp the great economic laws which
govern our industrial organizations." He pushed to extend
education to the poor, including free textbooks and free lunches,
if necessary. It was a source of anger to him that "In Winnipeg
today there are actually children growing up to be illiterates."

By June 1898, the paper's fifth year, Puttee could brag that
"we fearlessly advocate those things which make for the good
of the whole people." He called it a "zealous voice, eager in
upholding right against wrong and social equality." The *Voice*,
he extolled, "exposes with fearlessness and independence of

spirit. We fear no foe. We dread no party. We champion the rights of the people. We hate injustice, and we shall declaim against the oppression of the masses by the classes 'even though the heavens fall'."

It sounded like a speech and perhaps it was the beginnings of one. The following year, Puttee was already planning to run in a federal by-election set for January 1900. He believed fervently in the notion that the labour movement could only make good on its promise of social change if it gained political power. To that end, he put his name forward as the labour candidate and in a surprise upset, after a ballot recount, he was elected. He took up temporary residence in Ottawa's Cecil Hotel, then was re-elected in the general election that November. After 30 years of trying, labour had won its first seat in the federal Parliament.

Puttee's victory made him one of the youngest members of Parliament at 32 years of age and gave him access to the power about which he had done so much editorializing in the Voice. But it also brought him trouble. Some say he was too willing to accept Liberal Party policies, and that he had compromised labour's principles by taking Liberal financial support to win the election. That displeased the hard-line socialists who had been his faithful readership. He regularly promoted the founding of a political party modelled on the British Labour Party, but in 1906 when Winnipeg's Independent Labour Party was formed, the socialists were again unhappy because the party was moderate. They were especially insulted when even the word socialist was left out of the party's name.

There may have been some truth to the criticism that Puttee had gone soft. Although the socialist debate continued to fill the Voice even after the election, it slowly tapered off. Puttee continued to influence the editorial policy of the paper while he served as an MP, and perhaps the practicalities of political power had knocked some of the socialist wind out of the Voice's sails. Still, Puttee sought to practice in politics what he preached in his editorials.

For him, labour papers were "the sentinels that guard our interests and sound the note of warning upon the approach of danger; the champion that protects our principles in the face of every attack; and the guides that direct and aid us with judicious counsel in the hour of need." He took those words as his credo in other endeavours as well, including campaigns for worker's compensation, family allowances and public ownership of railways.

He lasted as an MP until the 1904 election, when the baggage he carried from his rumoured alliance with the Liberal Party proved to be his undoing. He failed to regain his seat when his opponents conducted a gossip campaign, talking of unidentified "revolutionists" and "assassins" who supposedly supported his re-election. The talk, especially comments by former labour council president and Liberal stalwart John Appleton, hurt him politically. Nor had it helped that his replacement at the *Voice* had been noted socialist J.T. Stott. The rumours were false, of course. Puttee was always more of a liberal reformer than a socialist. In later years, he would be an outspoken critic of the radical Industrial Workers of the World. But the gossip succeeded in sending him back to his editor's desk full-time.

In 1906, Puttee, Gus Pingle and a business-minded Conservative named J.F. Mitchell formed a new company to publish the paper. Mitchell was popular with working people and eventually became a member of the Legislative Assembly where he fought for a worker's compensation act. He also owned a two-storey building that the *Voice* proprietors could use and the company quickly expanded into the book and job-printing field as well as the photography business.

Puttee continued to edit the paper and Pingle sold ads, but it was always a losing proposition. Despite many attempts to gain subscription support, including free book offers, Puttee could not bring in enough to keep the paper going. The working population would happily read the new assortment of articles by politicos, faddists and cranks, which once included a flat earth exponent, but Puttee could not build circulation higher than the 5,000 he had reached by 1914.

Finally, after steering the paper through the war years, even during 1916 when he became a member of the board of control and in 1917 and 1918 when he held a city council seat, he gave up the helm. Apparently, by then his editorial policies, including his position on the 1918 civic workers' strike, had alienated much of Winnipeg's labour establishment. The paper was forced to cease publication.

When he died at 89 years of age in 1957, *Canadian Labour*, the organ of the newly founded Canadian Labour Congress, praised Puttee. "He was a quiet and unassuming man," the article said, "and much of the social legislation for which he fought vigorously is now largely taken for granted."

But in the late 1890s, the future passage of bits and pieces of key social legislation was far from the minds of many labour reformers and radicals. For them the stakes were much higher and the potential winnings much sweeter. If socialism won out—and the possibility seemed bright at the time—the social welfare of the entire country would be theirs to decide.

10

For the Masses Against the Classes

The ink was hardly dry on the first edition of *Citizen and Country* when the Post Office pulled the plug in March 1898. The new Toronto tabloid was "an advertising medium," according to postal authorities, and therefore did not qualify for special mailing privileges. But there was something strange about the whole meddlesome affair.

Only about five per cent of the Saturday weekly's eight pages were taken up with the revenue-generating ads. Obviously that wasn't what really bothered the bureaucrats and the Ottawa politicians. More likely, their problem was that the ads were for social reform books which regularly criticized government policies. When 30,000 copies of the new "Journal of Social, Moral and Economic Reform" arrived at the Toronto postal terminal that spring, the order to reject them had already been passed down from the federal capital.

Editor George Wrigley was livid. "Still-born" was how he described the first attempt to circulate his new paper. Undeterred, the veteran labour and social reform activist persisted and eventually mailed out an unprecedented 200,000 copies of the two-cent paper. He and a "comrade" had invested "nearly $5,000" in the new enterprise and they were not about to be stopped by bureaucratic red tape. Nor was Wrigley willing to accept the Ontario government's refusal to grant his Social Progress Company a publishing charter. The provincial authorities insisted that the joint stock company, with $20,000 in assets, had to change its name. Never afraid of a good fight, Wrigley refused to comply. He had the solid backing of company president Reverend Elliot S. Rowe and manager G. Weston Wrigley, the editor's son, and eventually the charter was his.

"Wrigley is a name that should be well known to every man in this country that pretends to be intelligently interested in social reform," Authur Puttee wrote in introducing the paper to readers of the *Voice* in Winnipeg. And, indeed, the man who would later be described by his son as "Canada's leading exponent of socialism" was no stranger to movement activists.

The *Citizen and Country* editor, who had first entered the newspaper business as editor of the Wallaceburg *Record*, was no stranger to public controversy, either. In fact, he had earned a reputation as one of the labour press warlords of the 1880s. As Chapter 5 describes, Wrigley had squared off with editors of other Knights of Labour weeklies in the summer of 1886. They charged that he was using boiler plate or pre-packaged material produced by scab labour in his St. Thomas, Ontario, labour paper, the *Canada Labour Courier*.

The dispute broadened in scope when the *Courier* editor had a spat with A.B. Ingram, a local labour candidate, and publicly withdrew his support for the Conservative Ingram. The local Knights assembly responded by boycotting the *Courier* and suspending Wrigley from the order for six months. The action spelled an end to the paper, but its founder remained unrepentent.

He moved on to London, Ontario, where he got a job with the *London Advertiser*. The paper, with its Knights sympathies, was a printing mecca for several of the best social reform journals of the early 1890s. The *Industrial Banner* was produced there, for example, and Wrigley himself used the company to print his new weekly, the *Canada Farmer's Sun*.

Still smarting from the labour movement boycott, the strong-willed social activist had turned to the temperance movement, editing the *Royal Templar* in Hamilton for a time. Then he found a new spiritual home with the farmers' movement, particularly a group called the Patrons of Industry. He started the *Farmer's Sun* in the spring of 1892 while still in London, but by 1893 he moved to Toronto where he published the *Sun* through the mid-1890s as an organ of the Patrons.

In the fall of 1895, Wrigley split the *Sun* in two. He reasoned that the *Sun* could continue to serve the interests of farmers exclusively, while a new paper, *Brotherhood Era*, would cater to trade unionists in an "urbanized" setting. For a short period, the new labour paper carried a full page of Toronto Trades and Labour Council news in hopes of attracting official support, but the reasoning was apparently faulty. Seven months after it started, the new paper was folded into the back pages of the *Sun*. In 1898, the ailing *Sun* was taken over by that old labour adversary, Goldwin Smith, who changed its name to the *Weekly Sun* and began contributing a controversial column under the pen-name Bystander.

Wrigley, longing to be back in the thick of labour movement struggles, believed deeply in the value of various social forces combining their efforts into one strong drive for change. He was aware of the problems that had been encountered in previous attempts to get farmers and labour together on any question for very long. Also, some labour advocates had undying memories of Wrigley's battles with the Knights of St. Thomas. J.G. Kilt, the editor of *Capital Siftings*, the Ottawa labour paper, was one of them, and he was not about to accept Wrigley back into the fold. The *Sun* "is doing its utmost to swim in harmony with labour," Kilt wrote. "It is, of course, somewhat at sea with regard to lines upon which labour men like to see a newspaper . . . run." Then he stuck the knife in and twisted. "Probably the farmers did not notice the predominance of the coarse boiler-plate in the Patron sheet. Labour men have, however, and the talented editor should not disparage his columns with this out-of-date trash."

Despite such naysayers, Wrigley was determined to show that different social movements could find common cause. His grand idea matured to the point where he was ready to test it out through the founding of *Citizen and Country*. The new paper would embody most of the causes of the labour movement, combining them with other social issues "affecting the best interests of the People." The glue that would hold them all together was socialism. At the outset, the editor espoused Christian or utopian socialism.

It was an eclectic vision, one whose time had apparently come. It was infrequent at first, appearing only semi-monthly, then finally going weekly. Recalling his own ups and downs, Wrigley advised readers with a line under the *Citizen and Country* banner to "Support a principle if it be right, even though it be not popular." He also highlighted the new paper's slogan: " 'Tis wisdom's law, the perfect code. By love inspired; From him on whom is much bestowed is much required." By avoiding the taint of a single, and often viciously sectarian social movement, Wrigley could proudly announce at the end of the first year that "Six thousand papers are now sent weekly to business and professional men, farmers and workingmen."

As the official organ of the Direct Legislation League of Canada, *Citizen and Country* added a new slogan to its banner: "Direct legislation [plebiscites, referenda] is the common denominator for all fractional reforms." Space was provided for the discussion of other political and social routes to reform as well, and the paper was soon calling for the abolition of the Senate, a proposal that was favourably received by many labour advocates.

Committed to his coalition-building ideal, Wrigley divided the paper into columns, one for each of the movements he supported. "The Brotherhood of Man" catered to Christian socialists. Then came "The Land Monopoly" produced by the Toronto Single Tax Association, "Banking and Currency" for currency reformers, "Public Ownership" for economic reformers, and "Electoral Reform" for supporters of universal suffrage and labour representation in the legislatures. But socialism was to become the mainstay of the paper. Little by little all the reform movements boiled down to one single challenge for Wrigley: the ultimate change from capitalism to a socialist system.

As the official organ of the Canadian Socialist League, the paper brought readers news of Henry George's single tax, Laurence Gronlund's co-operative commonwealth, and Daniel DeLeon's Socialist Labour Party in the United States. For a time, all the socialist tendencies of the era fit under the roof of Christian socialism and Wrigley devoted much space to its support. His headlines reveal his avid interest: "The Church and Sociology," "The Social Crisis and the Silent Church," "Preachers Discuss Socialism," "Socialism vs. Christian Socialism."

Eventually, the paper shed the Christian element from its socialism as it made its bid to become the main "Toronto reform journal." Before long, the Toronto Trades and Labour Council conferred its blessing on the paper, an endorsement that Wrigley coveted and intended to honour. Having been once burnt by the house of labour, he was not about to make the same mistake twice. When it came to the paper's coverage of women's issues, for example, the *Citizen and Country* editor was right in line with the policies of the Dominion Trades and Labour Congress. At its 1899 convention, the council had adopted a motion calling for the abolition of women from heavy industry, and Wrigley seemed to have no problem falling into step with it.

On the one hand, he sympathized with their lack of a vote. *"Citizen and Country* stands for woman's suffrage," he wrote in a front-page column, "and not even the fact that women, like men, are too often indescribably foolish can diminish our ardour for equal suffrage of the sexes." But when it came to women workers, Canada's national socialist weekly was all for pushing them out of the factories and back into the kitchen.

The paper also fell easily into step with organized labour's position on the Chinese immigration question. But unlike many of its predecessors, it took a more enlightened view of the issue. "The disastrous effect of Chinese wages on Canadian wage workers is not to be charged to the unfortunate Chinese at all," wrote the pseudonymous author Heterodox Economics. "The responsibility for that lies with Canadian and British employers, whose patriotism does not rise above profit seeking and never stops to consider soul crushing." The columnist noted with disgust the "infamous abuse of unfortunate Chinese victims of Canadian capitalists, supported at the Dominion ballot boxes by trade unionists who fawn and toady to that class whose administration . . . is the cause of evils charged to the Chinese."

It was a progressive view and one that Wrigley applied to other minorities in articles such as the one entitled "A Champion of Negroes." On the volatile Chinese issue, he must have sounded like a heretic to a movement which had hurled abuse at the oriental worker for more than two decades. Again, Wrigley was the black sheep. Yet he sought compromise wherever he sensed it might bring parties together in the fight for social change.

Similarly, he saw support for temperance as part of an over-all effort to encourage sweeping social changes. In the spirit of coalition that had inspired the founding of *Citizen and Country*, Wrigley recommended a merger of temperance organizations into a "Temperance Trust."

Wrigley took a different road in other labour causes as well. His weekly strongly backed the shorter hours movement, calling first for a "Nine-hour Workday," then falling into line with the other labour reformers who were already pushing for eight hours. Education was another Wrigley cause and he showered praise on Ontario's free library system, noting that the number of libraries had increased several hundredfold by 1898.

The editor also urged "Homes for the People." He lamented the lack of safer workplaces in a story on the death of a young worker who had been mutilated by a factory ripsaw. And he counselled working families to improve their health care, offering hope by announcing a cure for cancer, with "Positive Proof of Its Efficacy."

Since his days at the *Canada Labour Courier*, he had always been willing to stray from conventional wisdom, but in one case he held to the straight and narrow path of his journalistic brethren. The controversial editor was as rigorous as any of his predecessors in his condemnation of the "great unwashed partisan press." "It is hard to determine which is the more contemptible," he wrote, "the editor without brains of his own or the penny-a-liner who does the bidding of political bosses and endeavours to manufacture public opinion."

To the Winnipeg *Voice* and other contemporaries, *Citizen and Country* was "ably edited" and always prepared to discuss the "many reform problems that the press generally fears to handle." And like *Voice* editor Puttee, Wrigley accepted the aid of the country's best social commentators. Phillips Thompson's byline occasionally popped up, as did that of T.A. Foreman who also wrote for the *Voice* and the *Industrial Banner*. J.W. Bengough, editor of the satirical weekly *Grip*, submitted political cartoons commenting on the need for Senate reform, the party press, taxation and the nationalist fear of a takeover by Uncle Sam.

But the main attraction of *Citizen and Country* was its devotion to the cause of socialism. By 1900, the paper's subtitle had changed to "Canada's National Advocate of Trades Unionism and Socialism." Its slogan changed to "For the masses against social conditions that perpetuate the classes." And Wrigley began to contemplate moving the paper to Vancouver where a radical new wing of the labour movement was flexing its muscles.

It might be true, as some historians suggest, that only a small minority of western Canadian workers were interested in socialist agitation. Most of them worked long, hard hours in the mines and forests of the booming western hinterland and had free time for little else other than settling their families into the new wilderness. Still, Wrigley, whose paper claimed that 15 per cent of its subscribers were in British Columbia, saw the west as fertile ground for *Citizen and Country*'s socialist message.

Heated debates were already taking place in the west as immigrants from Britain discussed the tenets of Fabian socialism in logging camps. Migrant workers from the United States also brought their brand of socialism to the camps and the mines. Marxist ideas were circulated by word of mouth as workers from eastern Europe arrived in the attendant boom towns that were sprouting up.

In 1899, Wrigley toured the west with the Canadian Press Association. He had witnessed the conditions under which many of the migrants worked and he envisaged the growth of a unique radicalism. As historian Ross A. McCormack notes, "Socialist propaganda found its most eager audience among miners in British Columbia and Alberta and among low-status eastern European workers." Wrigley was eager to plunge into the debate.

There was already competition from other labour editors who sought the endorsement of the western labour movement. The *B.C. Workman* began publishing in early 1899, and soon earned the respect of the movement. The eight-page tabloid claimed to be "a slave to no party," and was endorsed by the Victoria Trades and Labour Council. The five-cent Saturday paper boasted that council members "were highly pleased" with the "live labour organ."

The *Workman* covered the gamut of issues, including women's rights, shorter hours, and the oriental labour issue. In this case, the Japanese bore the brunt of labour's anger. The paper provided coverage of socialistic communes like B.C.'s Ruskin Colony and the communal lifestyle of some newly arrived Russian emigrés calling themselves Doukhobors or spirit wrestlers. But for a broader view of social reform, the *Workman* recommended that its readers also subscribe to *Citizen and Country*.

With this support, Wrigley stepped up his plans to transplant his paper to the west coast. He was urged on by his old comrade, Reverend Rowe, who had blazed the trail. The avid Christian socialist had moved to B.C. and by mid-1900 was organizing Canadian Socialist League branches and preaching the social gospel to his Victoria congregation. By this time the younger Wrigley had taken a leadership role in founding the league and was playing a greater editorial role at *Citizen and Country*. He had learned many of the tricks of the trade from helping his father publish the *Farmer's Sun* years before, and could be counted on to handle affairs in Ontario.

When Wrigley Sr. finally moved the paper to B.C. in June 1902, he had already struck a deal with R. Parameter Pettipiece, publisher of the Ferguson (later Lardeau) *Eagle*, a labour paper serving the mining communities of the ore-rich Slocan Valley in B.C.'s southern interior. Pettipiece had sold the *Eagle* in March and moved to Vancouver. The two socialists met and Wrigley agreed that Pettipiece could buy a share of *Citizen and Country*. They renamed it the *Canadian Socialist*, and on July 5, 1902, it replaced the *Eagle* as the official organ of the Socialist Party of Canada.

But there was a new kind of socialism growing out of the working-class communities on Vancouver Island and in the B.C. interior. It was a Marxist socialism which had little time for the utopian socialism espoused by the Christian reformers. The Western Federation of Miners and the Industrial Workers of the World (the famed Wobblies) were organizing the west and promoting the new socialism. In late 1899, the Rossland *Industrial World* became the official organ of the miners' federation and began to educate workers in socialist principles.

As the new century settled in, the rift between Christian socialists and Marxists was paralleled by a more dangerous one for Canadian trade unionism. The Dominion Trades and Labour Congress, founded in 1883, was the official house of labour, and it had long adopted a comparatively moderate political stance. A major split developed between the eastern labourites and the western socialists, and eventually led to a bitter struggle between those who supported 'pure and simple' unionism and the socialists.

Wrigley played a major role in the debate and watched over Canadian socialism's transformation from a utopian socialist to Marxist philosophy. But his stay in the west was inexplicably cut short. One possibility was his failing health; he had apparently suffered a stroke around 1900. By September 1902 he had sold his share in the Social Progress Company (including a printing plant) to Pettipiece and moved to Victoria to join his old friend Rowe and become an American Labour Union organizer on Vancouver Island. Later that same year, he was back in Toronto publishing yet another reform journal, this time a monthly broadsheet called *Social Justice*. Its masthead stated that it stood for "justice for the underdog in the economic struggle, and eventually an equality of opportunity by the removal of all special privileges and franchises." Wrigley used the new paper to call for a "peaceful revolution."

Meanwhile, as the various socialist factions battled it out in the west during the first decades of the new century, *Citizen and Country* fuelled the debate. After its short stint as the *Canadian Socialist*, Pettipiece changed its name to the *Western Socialist*. Then in spring 1903, the paper merged with the Nanaimo *Clarion*, a labour paper which had connections to the United Brotherhood of Railway Employees. What emerged was yet another name change, this time to the *Western Clarion*. The new incarnation of *Citizen and Country* appeared as a tri-weekly on May 7, 1903, and published until it was suspended in 1918. Two years later, as the world picked up the pieces in the aftermath of the Great War, it was resurrected. It had missed the culmination of social agitation that had occurred at Winnipeg in 1919, when unions shut down the Manitoba capital in the famous general strike. It came to life again at about the same time as the Communist Party of Canada was being founded in a barn just outside Guelph, Ontario, in 1921.

When the paper finally succumbed in 1925, the power struggle between the socialists and the labourites in the Canadian labour movement was once again warming up for renewed battles in the 1930s and 1940s. By then workers looked to new labour newspapers to help them understand an increasingly complex world, one that would soon be at war again.

Conclusion

The Spirit of Solidarity

At the height of the British Columbia labour movement's fight against former premier Bill Bennett's Draconian fiscal restraint program, a feisty little newspaper was launched to do battle for B.C. workers. It was christened *Solidarity Times*, after the Solidarity Coalition that had been set up to counter Bennett's rigid measures.

It was fall 1983, but in many ways the tabloid weekly harkened back to a tradition started long before. In format and language it was not at all like the paper R.M. Moore had launched back in 1842 as the backdrop to the founding of a Canadian labour press. In content it didn't resemble the editorial style of Isaac Buchanan's *Workingman's Journal* of 1894 or the later pioneer labour papers. But in other ways it was part of the same family of independent, spirited journals of labour and social reform.

Like its ancestors, *Solidarity Times* carried paid advertising, appeared weekly and charged a cover price (50 cents). Despite its slightly overdone 'punk' image, the new paper had spunk and lots of it. It attracted 2,000 paid subscribers and sold another 2,000 copies weekly on newsstands. It provided plenty of space for critical debate in the letters section. In short, it was everything critics had been clamouring for since the demise of an independent labour press.

More than 80 years earlier, the turn of a new century had brought with it numerous attempts to continue the vibrant and outspoken movement press of the late 19th century. Plenty of weekly newspapers like the *Times* would come and go as the country struggled in vain to live up to Prime Minister Wilfrid Laurier's famous line about the 20th century belonging to Canada.

Leading up to the First World War, the *Industrial Banner* continued to publish in London and later in Toronto. The *Voice* served Winnipeg labour. *Citizen and Country* re-emerged as the *Western Clarion* out on the west coast. The old labour press war horses of the 1890s were joined by papers like Hugh Peat's *Saskatchewan Labour's Realm* founded in Regina in 1907. In 1908, socialists read *Cotton's Weekly* in Cowansville, Quebec, and Ed Stephenson ably issued the *Lance* to Toronto workers who had been formerly served by the *Toiler* and then the *Tribune*.

In 1909, the *Eastern Labour News*, edited by J.C. Merrill, began servicing the Atlantic region from Moncton, New Brunswick. By 1911, R.P. Pettipiece, one of George Wrigley's partners on *Citizen and Country*, had started the *B.C. Federationist* in Vancouver. In 1912, William G. Newald started the *Canadian Labour Leader* in Sydney, Nova Scotia, and Samuel L. Landress roused the memory of the *Palladium of Labour* with the Hamilton *Labour News*. In 1916, the Social Democratic Party founded *Canadian Forward*, replacing *Cotton's Weekly*, and Montreal workers saw the first edition of *Le Monde Ouvrier*.

As the First World War ended, editors continued to search for the magic formula that would give their papers credibility and the subscription support a publication needs to survive and flourish. C.W. Lunn, who had started *Lunn's Weekly* in 1911, edited the *Eastern Federationist* (later the *Worker's Weekly*) in New Glasgow, Nova Scotia. Vancouver socialists temporarily renamed the *Western Clarion* the *Red Flag*, then called it the *Indicator* before returning to the *Clarion*. William Ivens took over the *Voice* in Winnipeg, renaming it the *Western Labour News*. In 1919, Henry J. Roche edited the Edmonton *Free Press* (later *Alberta Labour News*), Ontario began seeing the *Canadian Labour Press*, and John Houston started the *One Big Union Bulletin*, filling it with news of the Winnipeg General Strike.

The Roaring Twenties and Dirty Thirties brought more labour papers, especially trade union newsletters and foreign-language labour journals. A literary/political monthly called the *Canadian Forum* also appeared in 1920, and with the founding of the Communist Party of Canada in 1921, came the *Worker* (later *Daily Clarion*). Co-operative movement publications continued to appear alongside those from the farmers' movement and various socialist and social democratic groupings. The Great Depression created a need for journals to serve the unemployed masses and those who moved into work camps to survive.

At the same time, Adolph Hitler and his Nazis prepared to bully the world into a new war, including a vicious prelude in the Spanish Civil War of the mid-1930s. Pacifist and anti-fascist news made its way into workers' homes. Trade union papers and labour-oriented political journals not unlike *Solidarity Times* reported on the famed Mackenzie-Papineau Battalion, the armed force of Canadian workers who fought against fascism in Spain.

Some of the papers had grown out of the Co-operative Commonwealth Federation or were inspired by the CCF's Regina Manifesto. After the Second World War and into the 1950s, internal feuding in the labour movement preoccupied the leadership and led to the McCarthyist purges of the period. Few new labour papers began. With the consolidation of the house of labour under the Canadian Labour Congress roof in 1956, and the founding of the New Democratic Party in 1961, existing labour papers focused more and more on purely union matters, on "bread and butter" issues as opposed to wide social concerns.

Throughout the late 1960s and early 1970s, the labour press made way for a vital new social reform press. It was made up of peace magazines, underground newspapers, feminist newsletters and a parade of other movement publications. In many ways, *Solidarity Times* looked to them for its inspiration more than it did to a labour press which had been largely transformed into rhetoric-spouting house organs. It didn't call itself a labour paper. Instead it was to be "politically independent." But the money came mostly from the B.C. Federation of Labour, a reality that would ultimately lead to the paper's premature demise.

Much of the content of the first issue appealed to the embattled provincial labour movement, especially the younger trade unionists. A think piece on Bennett's spring budget, for example, was headed "Let's spend the night together," after a song by the Rolling Stones rock group. An editorial cartoon showed eight rats, presumably cabinet ministers, eating away at a cheese called "basic democratic rights." The attractive tabloid also carried some sports and entertainment coverage.

It seemed too good to be true, and after nine driven issues, the B.C. Federation popped the balloon. It had donated about $90,000 to keep the bold new weekly alive, but the leadership had decided that enough was enough. "We were politically under the thumb of the B.C. Fed," said editor Stan Persky, a writer and activist who had edited a similar paper in northern B.C. with some success. "Most of the executive saw *Solidarity Times* as a scandalous and dangerous idea." When one executive member angrily suggested that even letters should be censored, Persky, like some of the pioneers who had once gone to jail to defend freedom of expression, argued that "a newspaper should not be viewed as traitorous every time it publishes a letter which is somewhat critical of the labour movement." But his protest fell on deaf ears. The federation pulled the plug on funding and *Solidarity Times* was history.

For Skip Hambling, the B.C. paper must have been a dream come true. As the Ottawa stringer for *Labour News*, the national news service that in 1981 had replaced the Co-operative Press Associates service begun back in the 1940s, he had a front-row seat from which to observe the modern trade union press. He had not been impressed. When *Solidarity Times* came along, it had something that he felt today's union press lacks— heart. Union editors see working on a labour paper as "just a job," he noted, when what is called for is a lot of emotional energy to make the papers sing.

Solidarity Times, although it made plenty of mistakes, promised to do just that. But the labour movement, which could offer the stability and potential readership that were lacking in other movements, was not ready for what Persky and his team of young journalists would roll out of their typewriters. A more conservative climate had swept over North America since the modern heyday of radical newspapers in the 1960s. The mood had filtered through to the movement, making it less receptive to the editorial brew Persky had concocted.

Even if union editors wanted to spearhead a labour press renaissance partly inspired by the short-lived popularity of *Solidarity Times*, they have learned to live with the fact that the labour press is not an all-consuming passion with union leaders. They know there is little hope that labour leaders would agree to cover the cost of hiring full-time editors and devoting more of the budget to original writing, production and distribution.

Many of them also know that the modern union press has not sustained the vitality or the significance of its labour press ancestry. Today's union press has a captive audience; almost all publications are sent free (as a benefit of union dues) to at least a percentage of members. And despite rumours of their impending demise, unionized workers add up to more than a third of the workforce in Canada. But even with the huge potential readership, union editors are painfully aware that the modern union press is not a serious player in the key debates of the union movement or the country.

Critics have suggested that part of the problem is the lack of a spirit of competition both within the union press and between it and commercial publications. Some union editors counter that union papers should not and cannot compete with the commercial press, as they tried to do in the pioneer years. But they can "raise the consciousness of workers," and inform the small group of activists who regularly read the union press.

To do this well means finding out how conscious workers already are. But many union editors do not survey readers to determine their information needs. They fear that readers would be highly critical of the lack of investigative features, uncensored letters pages, rank-and-file opinion columns and hard news about the movement.

Some union editors see their publications as "puff pieces," uncritical house organs with no room for anyone who thinks they are working at serious labour journalism. They do not see their jobs as being crusaders for some noble cause, as did many of the pioneers. Instead, the main purpose of the union paper for them is to "promote the views of the union."

Other union editors say the real job is to inform members of their rights using facts, not rhetoric. But many union papers tend to emphasize the union's merits at the expense of providing members with hard facts about the benefits of the movement. There is often a poor balance between coverage of what members are doing and the activities of elected officers. In most cases, the latter gets the lion's share of the coverage.

Perhaps the biggest problem of all is that no one seems to read the modern union press except the leadership and the union faithful—the already converted. It is not a new problem. The pioneer papers faced the same difficulty and, as we have seen, were in a constant circulation war with the penny dailies. Today, union papers compete with the latest crop of zany sitcoms, blood-spurting cop shows and steamy mini-series on television. They also have to contend with an increasing number of 'infotainment' style news programs that are often willing to sacrifice content for style and a pretty face.

"Parochialism is one of the biggest enemies" of the labour press, says Angus Ricker, like Hambling a former editor of the *Commonwealth*, the New Democratic Party's Saskatchewan newspaper. "Pictures of brother so-and-so and the results of the union elections don't make for a very interesting paper," he adds. Labour papers should report on the union, its position on the larger issues in society, as well as the industry, Ricker notes. "We live in a world. It's not just Local 634 or whatever."

When Ricker judged the Canadian Association of Labour Media awards in 1980, he gave top honours to the *Fisherman*. Then a fortnightly, it sold ads, charged a cover price and competed with other publications covering the fishing industry. Since readers have come to expect those things of a "real" newspaper, the *Fisherman* has built a credibility not enjoyed by most other union papers. Today, Ricker still calls it a "bible to the whole industry." He wonders why a "paper like that can't exist in every union."

John Clark, another CALM awards judge, observes that "If labour papers are not being read by the majority of union members, then the reason may be that the papers lack credibility." Clark argues that "our papers are so pro-union that many people (including our own members) regard them as propaganda." He suggests that "perhaps what is needed is a more objective approach. Perhaps it is time for labour editors to press for greater independence."

Not everyone agrees with those assessments. Some union editors say that despite union budget restraints there's been a steady increase in the quality of labour papers. But if some union journalism is devoid of energy and vitality, they argue, it is partly because many editors are forced to get pre-publication clearance from leaders. This stifles any sense of responsibility and pride they might have in what they publish. Others say that editors, often fearing for their jobs, are already engaged in their own form of self-censorship.

For some editors, the job of union papers is to expose management delinquencies and reflect union policy. To them, the union paper is where labour's side of the story gets told, but that does not always include printing what workers say about their unions, positive or negative. Balance is not relevant. Although supportive, they see no need for union papers to try to emulate respected critical journals sympathetic to labour such as the *New Statesman* in Britain or *In These Times* and the *Guardian* in the United States.

Many union editors agree that union papers spend too much time reporting on conferences, don't challenge the membership with good writing and don't work hard enough at getting photos and stories about people in the workplace. Few of them think the union press can break news, but they suggest that papers should attempt to "popularize current issues," making them accessible to rank and file members.

The one big no-no of the modern labour press—and the kiss of death for *Solidarity Times*—is movement self-criticism. Some editors don't believe the labour press can serve its own interests or the broader interest by criticizing the movement. Others say editors shouldn't go looking for labour-bashing material, but if a member wants to say something critical about the union let them do it on the letters page. Still, few critical letters are published in the modern union press.

Why is it such heresy to suggest that union papers take a critically constructive look at their own movement? Part of the answer is that most editors and leaders feel the mass media already do a more than adequate job on that front. Indeed, to raise the issue of mainstream labour reporting with union editors is to invite a rash of angry commentary. Complaints of inaccuracies and biased coverage in the daily media are legion at CALM conventions, and many media critics argue that the anger is justified.

Unquestionably, the labour movement does not receive media coverage proportionate to its role in society. As John A. Hannigan concluded in the most recent study of Canadian labour reporting, it is in a "generally negative state." He found that while media owners don't dictate the way labour should be covered, they also do not provide the resources to improve coverage. "The labour reporter is still very much a marginal figure," Hannigan writes, "caught between management and labour and between sources and editors." He noted that most labour reporting is geared to strikes and that reporters find it difficult to write about working life outside dramatic workplace conflicts.

Globe and Mail labour reporter Lorne Slotnick agrees with some of the criticisms of the mainstream media and he praises some trade union publications. "Some local union papers are damn good," he says. "They are put out by one person who knows what's going on and can write about it for the rank and file. They are relevant." But he adds that many of the national union publications are "riddled with pictures of the president." Too many union papers "just hit you over the head with union leadership and the NDP." They don't do enough to help people understand why the union takes certain stands, he says, and they are too often satisfied to preach to the already converted. And the most telling comment of all: "You don't find many stories [story leads] in the labour press."

Like many others, Slotnick underlines the need for a new independent labour press that could provide professional coverage of labour news and have a strong influence in the world of labour affairs. But how much real influence could a revitalized labour press have? For part of the answer we must look to the pioneers. How much influence did the early labour press exert on opinion leaders of its day?

Part of the job of the dedicated pioneer labour editor was to reflect the working-class culture that accompanied the movement's political awakening. As the 19th century pressed on, labour's voices became a choir of social advocacy. As we have seen, labour editors worked feverishly to shape the workers' social and cultural attitudes.

"In the pages of well-known Hamilton-Toronto journals, such as the *Labour Union, Wage Worker, Trades Union Advocate, Canadian Labour Reformer*, and *Labour Advocate*, the culture was at its most vibrant and visible," according to historians Greg Kealey and Bryan Palmer. "The existence of other organs, from the voice of [Daniel] O'Donoghue, the *Labour Record*, to the St. Thomas *Canada Labour Courier*, edited by George Wrigley, a future farmers' advocate and socialist, through labour papers barely known to have existed—Ottawa's *Free Lance* and *Capital Siftings*, London's *Evening News* (issued in the midst of an 1884 strike), Brockville's *Equalizer*—demonstrated the scope and strength of the working-class presence in these years."

These papers reported on such cultural institutions as Labour Day parades, the neighbourhood pub where much heated discussion took place, and volunteer fire brigades which many community-spirited workers joined. There were articles on early workers' night schools called mechanic's institutes, fraternal societies with their famed oyster suppers, and the local baseball scene (some labour editors captained teams that challenged the local commerical press).

In its earnestness, the pioneer labour press hastened and sometimes hindered social progress. Sometimes an impassioned editor's howl would raise a public outcry or a politician's sympathy, although few laws were passed as a direct result of such complaints on behalf of Canadian workers.

But the pioneer editors did go beyond pure union concerns to scrutinize society as a whole. They cried out for better education, healthier and safer workplaces, an end to child labour, the establishment of old age security and equal pay for female factory labourers. They pleaded for full employment, improved housing, more job security, and a major assault on poverty. They advocated shorter working hours, temperance, co-operatives, political representation, unionization and even all-out revolution as ways to bring about social reforms.

They weren't always on the right side of the issue. As documented in this book, editors often lined up to cast racist aspersions in the direction of Chinese and Japanese immigrant labourers. And they often failed to provide a truly progressive view in the ongoing debate over the rights of women and children, a flaw that might have been overcome if there had been even a few female labour editors. Still, they played an essential role in keeping the issues high on the agenda of the new and struggling labour movement.

Modern-day critics of the pioneer papers argue that they had little influence on social affairs. They say Victorian labour periodicals were few in number and often miles off course in their appeal to workers. Circulations were often too small to save them from financial ruin. But like any opposition or alternative press, the audience can be much broader than its actual circulation figures would indicate. Many politicians, church leaders, pundits and labour critics combed the labour press looking for a shift in political attitudes or cultural trends. They also watched for reports of internal debates within the movement that would provide them with new insights.

It was in the pages of the pioneer labour press that labour commentators drafted the blueprint for a new society long cherished by the self-appointed champions of working people. The real value of these journals might have been the fact that they existed at all to provide the inspiration needed for the movement to carry on.

Here, labour and social reform advocates tested their ideas for change and debated the social issues and sweeping solutions to society's problems. These working papers of an intellectual radicalism laid the groundwork in many cases for future social legislation and a lasting third-party political system. Much of the credit for those feats rests with a handful of pioneering labour journalists.

As Kealey and Palmer write, despite their idiosyncracies, "these men attempted to move the class beyond economism, striving 'to take a broader and more comprehensive view of the entire subject of Labour Reform than is embodied in mere unionism'." It was only through the perseverance of a few devoted printers-turned-publishers—with some support from trade unions—that the labour press survived.

Media historian Paul Rutherford agrees. "These weeklies shaped the traditions of the working class in early industrial Canada and criticized, vociferously, the capitalist system which in so many ways seemed unjust to the labouring man." Rutherford concludes that the 19th-century labour and social reform press "added a new dimension to the already complex expression of the Canadian Mosaic."

Some say the early labour press occupied a far more significant position than all the factions and tendencies of the movement put together. In fact, it would seem that the movement was often staffed in large part by the people who published the labour journals. American historian Joseph R. Conlin suggests this was true of many early movements, including labour. The volunteer labour editor was often a union leader himself, adding to the editorial copy the high energy that comes with unswerving belief in a cause.

But whatever their primary motivations and however small their circulations, the pioneer labour press provided a forum for debate of popular ideas for social change. As Conlin notes, these papers, along with other radical journals, were "the most important single means of spreading the word." By identifying the issues and publishing the views of popular intellectuals, pioneer labour papers recorded the development of a working-class consciousness and presented an image of labour culture. They were the sounding boards for a little-explored radical tradition in Canadian history.

Was anybody listening to the 19th-century labour journalists? Yes, a few did listen. They carried some of the ideas for

social change into the next century as they became the politicians, labour advocates and labour journalists of a new era. A
young Winnipeg man named J.S. Woodsworth was among
those who read and drew inspiration from the labour press.
And there were others, less famous than the CCF founder,
who were also urged onward by these social voices of the
Canadian labour movement.

*   *   *   *   *

In the fall of 1988, B.C. workers were struggling against
even more difficult odds than they were five years earlier when
Solidarity Times came on the scene. Bill Bennett has gone and
in his place is the still more conservative Premier William Vander
Zalm. His changes to the province's labour laws, including the
replacement of the B.C. Labour Relations Board with the much
more powerful and unilateral Industrial Relations Commission,
have helped put the entire labour movement on a war footing
as never before. Indeed, the B.C. Federation of Labour has
asked affiliates to boycott the IRC in its continuing fight against
Bills 19 and 20, the new laws which labour leaders argue are
an attempt to shackle the labour movement. (Bill 19 severely
restricts free collective bargaining and Bill 20 virtually decerti-
fied the B.C. Teachers' Federation.)

In many ways, the B.C. situation is a litmus test for the
rest of the country. What the Social Credit government intro-
duces in an attempt to neutralize the labour movement is closely
watched by other governments. If it works there, they could
adopt similar measures in other provinces. And they could do
it in partnership with a Conservative federal government wedded
to the anti-labour policies of privatization, deregulation and a
free trade agreement with the United States that labour says
will create a heyday for free-enterprise capitalism, Americanize
the country and devastate the economy.

As for the death of *Solidarity Times* and the insular nature
of the union press, Canada's political magazines have worked
tirelessly to hold the fort. Magazines like Vancouver's *New
Directions*, for example, grew out of the Solidarity experience.
It joined *Our Times*, the defunct *Goodwin's*, *New Maritimes*, *This
Magazine*, *Briarpatch*, *Canadian Dimension* and other alternatives.
But good as they can be, none of these publications is a true
substitute for a weekly labour press.

Unfortunately, the prospects for such a rebirth do not seem bright even though there is a pivotal need for a new voice to speak on behalf of the broad Canadian labour movement. To its credit, the B.C. Federation of Labour has bounced back after the *Solidarity Times* fiasco. It recently launched a new television series to help fight the anti-labour Socred government. It is a bold move that may help bring the labour movement into the modern age of communications technology. The producers have even been told to solicit paid ads to pay for the series. So far, the accounts include Nissan, the Royal Bank and PetroCan, among others. It's a real breakthrough! But TV has never been the medium of labour. It has been a print-oriented movement since the beginning and it will take time—and big money—to develop quality TV programming to attract the vast potential audience represented by trade unionists.

In the meantime, perhaps what is needed are labour weeklies that will give voice and spirit to Canadian workers, a press that would enliven an embattled union movement as it pushes on into the 21st century. If such a press were launched, it would have much to learn from the successes and the critical mistakes of the pioneer labour press.

References

Traditionally, historians have scanned the labour press in search of accounts of leadership rivalries, reports on great strikes or the labour movement's official view on issues. Seldom have they viewed it as a social force which represented and often helped shape the opinions of a small but vocal group of labour advocates.

By contrast, as Viv Nelles noted in a *Saturday Night* magazine article, today's social historians have used the labour press to transform the "somewhat arid subject of labour history into a lively crossroads of debate and research on working-class institutions and culture."

Through the work of scholars like Greg Kealey and Bryan Palmer, for example, at least one all-but-forgotten social institution has gained some historical prominence. The works of these historians, listed below, portray the labour press as a principal player—an active voice—in labour's attempts to propagate its brand of social progress.

They are joined by other contributors, some of whom have studied the politics of the labour press or its literary heritage, some of whom have merely listed the names of labour newspapers. Some have been painstakingly well documented, others have been faulty.

Frank J. Watt's 1957 doctoral thesis "Radicalism in English-Canadian Literature Since Confederation" is an ideal starting point for research into the labour press. Robbins L. Elliott, in his 1947 Master's thesis, provided an early "annotated bibliography" of the labour press, but it contains some glaring errors which taint its usefulness.

Of course, the pioneer labour papers and social reform journals themselves provide the most illuminating look at 19th-century working-class life. However, the following materials are an excellent supplement to the primary sources.

Adams, R.J. (1979) *Education and Working Canadians*. Ottawa: Labour Canada.

Allen, Richard. (1971) *The Social Passion: Religion and Social Reform in Canada, 1914-28*. Toronto: University of Toronto Press.

Ames, Herbert Brown. (1972) *The City Below the Hill*. Toronto: University of Toronto Press.

Appleton, Paul Campbell. (1974) "The Sunshine and the Shade: Labour Activism in Central Canada, 1850-1860." Calgary: University of Calgary MA thesis.

Armitage, Andrew. (1975) *Social Welfare in Canada*. Toronto: McClelland and Stewart.

Aspinall, Arthur. (1949) *Politics and the Press*, 1780-1850. London: Home and Van Thal Ltd.

Avakumovic, Ivan. (1978) *Socialism in Canada: A Study of the CCF-NDP in Federal and Provincial Politics*. Toronto: McClelland and Stewart.

Bagnell, Kenneth. (1980) *The Little Immigrants: The Orphans Who Came to Canada*. Toronto: Macmillan.

Battye, John. (1979) "The Nine-Hour Pioneers: The Genesis of the Canadian Labour Movement." *Labour/Le Travailleur* 4:25-56.

Beaulieu, Andre; Hamelin, Jean. (1973) *La presse québecoise des origines à nos jours*, Volumes 1-5. Quebec City: Les presses de l'Université Laval.

Bell, John David. (1975) "The Social and Political Thought of the Labor Advocate." Kingston, Ontario: Queen's University MA thesis.

Bellamy, Edward. (1967) *Looking Backward*. Cambridge, Mass.: Belknap Press of Harvard University Press.

Berger, Carl. (1970) *The Sense of Power—Studies in the Ideas of Canadian Imperialism, 1867-1914*. Toronto: University of Toronto Press.

Bliss, Michael, ed. (1975) *League for Social Reconstruction*. Toronto: Social Planning for Canada, ' Jniversity of Toronto Press (The Social History of Canada series).

Boyce, George; Curran, James; Wingate, Pauline, eds. (1978) *Newspaper History from the Seventeenth Century to the Present Day*. London: Constable.

Briggs, Asa; Saville, John, eds. (1960) *Essays in Labour History*. London: Macmillan.

Bryden, Kenneth. (1974) *Old Age Pensions and Policy-Making in Canada*. Montreal and London: The Institute of Public Administration, McGill-Queen's University Press.

Buchanan, Isaac. Personal papers of Isaac Buchanan. Public Archives of Canada (Third Floor) 119 Volumes. Vol. 115 contains Vol. 1, No. 12 of *The Election News* (April 21, 1864) with an editorial announcing the *Workingman's Journal*.

Chan, Victor 0. (1949) "Canadian Knights of Labor with special reference to the 1880's." Montreal: McGill University MA thesis.

Cherwinski, Walter J. (1972) "Organized Labour in Saskatchewan: The TLC Years, 1905-1945." Edmonton: University of Alberta Ph.D. thesis.

Clarke, Phyllis. (undated) "The Politics of Labor: The Life and Times of Phillips Thompson." Toronto: University of Toronto political science essay.

Clark, Samuel Delbert. (1968) *The Developing Canadian Community*. Toronto: University of Toronto Press.

_____. (1942) *The Social Development of Canada*. Toronto: University of Toronto Press.

Coats, R.H. (1913) "The Labour Movement in Canada" in *Canada and Its Provinces* Vol. 9. Toronto: Dominion Industrial Development Publishers' Association of Canada Ltd.

Colquhoun, A.H.U. et. al. (1908) *A History of Canadian Journalism* in the several portions of the Dominion with a sketch of the Canadian Press Association. Toronto: Canadian Press Association.

Commons, John R. (1948) *The American Labor Press: An Annotated Directory*. Washington: American Council on Public Affairs.

Commons, John R. et. al. (1916) *Principles of Labor Legislation.* New York: Harper and Brothers.

Commons, John R. et. al. (1918) *History of Labor in the United States.* New York: Augustus M. Kelley, Publishers.

Conlin, Joseph R. (1974) *The American Radical Press, 1880-1960.* Westport, Conn.: Greenwood Press.

Connors, J.M. (undated) Draft biography of James Simpson. James Simpson Papers. Toronto: Baldwin Room, Metropolitan Toronto Library.

Cook, Ramsay. (1979) "Neglected Pine Blasters." *Canadian Literature,* No. 81.

_____. (1975) "The Professor and the Prophet of Unrest." *Transactions of the Royal Society of Canada,* Fourth Series, Vol. XIII.

Cranfield, G.A. (1978) *The Press and Society: From Caxton to Northcliffe.* London: Longman Group Ltd.

Creighton, Donald. (1943) "George Brown, Sir John A. Macdonald, and the 'Workingman'." *Canadian Historical Review,* Vol. XXIV No. 4.

Cross, Michael S. (1973) "The Shiners' War: Social Violence in the Ottawa Valley in the 1830s." *Canadian Historical Review,* Vol. LIV, No. 1.

_____. (1971) "Stony Monday, 1849: The Rebellion Losses Riots in Bytown." *Ontario History,* Vol. LXIII, No. 3.

Davis, W.L. (1930) "A History of the Early Labor Movement in London, Ontario." London: University of Western Ontario MA thesis.

Dahl, Folke. (undated) "Amsterdam: Cradle of English Newspapers." (city and publisher unknown).

Dewalt, Bryan Thomas. (1985) "Arthur W. Puttee: Labourism and Working-Class Politics in Winnipeg, 1894-1918." Winnipeg: University of Manitoba MA thesis.

Drummond, Robert. (1926) *Recollections and Reflections of a Former Trade Union Leader.* Stellarton, N.S.: Provincial Workman's Association.

Dulles, Foster Rhea. (1966) *Labor in America: A History.* New York: Thomas Y. Crowell Co.

Elliott, Robbins Leonard. (1947) "A Study of the Canadian Labour Press, 1867-1947." Toronto: University of Toronto MA thesis.

Filler, Louis. (1976) *The Muckrakers.* University Park and London: Pennsylvania State University Press.

Finkel, Alvin. (1979) *Business and Social Reform in the Thirties.* Toronto: James Lorimer and Co.

Firth, Edith. (1961) *Early Toronto Newspapers, 1793-1867.* Toronto: Baxter Publishing Co. and Toronto Public Library.

Forsey, Eugene. (1982) *Trade Unions in Canada, 1812-1902.* Toronto: University of Toronto Press.

_____. (1947) "A Note on the Dominion Factory Bills of the Eighteen-Eighties." *Canadian Journal of Economics and Political Science,* Vol. 13, No. 4.

_____. (undated) Eugene Forsey Papers. Ottawa: Public Archives of Canada.

French, Goldwin. (1962) *Parsons and Politics: The Role of the Wesleyan Methodists in Upper Canada and the Maritimes from 1780-1855.* Toronto: Ryerson Press.

Gagan, David. (1981) *Hopeful Travellers: Families, Land, and Social Change in Mid-Victorian Peel County, Canada West.* Toronto: University of Toronto Press.

Garlin, Sender. (1976) *John Swinton: American Radical (1829-1901)*. New York: Occasional Paper No. 20, American Institute for Marxist Studies.

George, Henry. (1884) *Social Problems*. London: Kegan Paul, Trench and Co.

——————. (1966) *Progress and Poverty*. London: Hogarth Press.

Gibbney, H.J. (1975) *Labor in Print: A guide to the people who created a labor press in Australia between 1850 and 1939*. Canberra: Australian Dictionary of Biography, Australian National University.

Goldwater, Walter. (1964) *Radical Periodicals in America 1890-1950*. New Haven, Conn.: Yale University Press.

Goodwyn, Lawrence. (1976) *Democratic Promise: The Populist Movement in America*. New York: Oxford University Press.

Graff, Harvey J. (1979) *The Literacy Myth: Literacy and Social Structure in the Nineteenth-Century City*. New York: Academic Press.

Guest, Dennis. (1980) *The Emergence of Social Security in Canada*. Vancouver: University of British Columbia Press.

Hann, Russell G. (1977) "An Early Canadian Theorist." *Bulletin of the Committee on Canadian Labour History*, No. 4.

Hann, Russell G.; Kealey, Greg; Kealey, Linda; Warrian, Peter. (1973) *Primary Sources in Canadian Working Class History*. Kitchener, Ont.: Dumont Press.

Hardman, J.S.; Neufeld, Maurice F., eds. (1951) *The House of Labor—Internal Operations of American Unions*. Westport, Conn.: Greenwood Press.

Harper, J. Russell. (1961) *Historical Directory of New Brunswick Newspapers and Periodicals*. Fredericton: University of New Brunswick.

Harrison, Brian. (1971) *Drink and the Victorians: The Temperance Question in England, 1815-1872*. Pittsburgh: University of Pittsburgh Press.

Harrison, Royden; Wollven, Gillian B.; Duncan, Robert. (1977) *The Warwick Guide to British Labour Periodicals, 1790-1970*. Sussex, Eng.: Harvester Press/Humanities Press.

Harrison, Stanley. (1974) *Poor Man's Guardians*. London: Lawrence and Wishart.

Hobsbawn, Eric J. (1979) *Labouring Men: Studies in the History of Labour*. London: Weidenfeld and Nicholson.

——————. (1959) *Primitive Rebels: Studies in Archaic Forms of Social Movement in the 19th and 20th Centuries*. Manchester, Eng.: Manchester University Press.

Hollis, Patricia. (1970) *The Pauper Press: A Study in Working-Class Radicalism of the 1930s*. London: Oxford University Press.

Horowitz, Gad. (1968) *Canadian Labour in Politics*. Toronto: University of Toronto Press.

Hurtig, Mel. (1985) *Canadian Encyclopedia*. Edmonton: Hurtig Publishers.

Industrial Banner Scrapbook and Daybook. (1891) Includes correspondence, subscription receipts, editor's salary, advertising revenues and sales commissions. London, Ont.: Regional Collection, University of Western Ontario Library.

Innis, Harold A. (1972) *Empire and Communications*. Toronto: University of Toronto Press.

Jamieson, Stuart. (1957) *Industrial Relations in Canada*. Toronto: Macmillan.

Johnson, Leo A. (1973) *History of the County of Ontario, 1615-1875*. Whitby, Ont.: Corporation of the County of Ontario.

Johnson, Ross Alfred. (1975) "No Compromise—No Political Trading: The Marxian Socialist Tradition in British Columbia." Vancouver: University of British Columbia Ph.D. thesis.

Jones, Andrew; Rutman, Leonard. (1981) *In the Children's Aid: J.J. Kelso and Child Welfare in Ontario*. Toronto: University of Toronto Press.

Katz, Michael B. (1975) *The People of Hamilton, Canada West: Family and Class in a Mid-Nineteenth-Century City*. Cambridge, Mass.: Harvard University Press.

Katz, Michael B.; Mattingly, Paul, eds. (1975) *Education and Social Change: Themes from Ontario's Past*. New York: New York University Press.

Kealey, Greg. (1973) *Canada Investigates Industrialism* (Report of the Royal Commission on the Relations of Labour and Capital, 1889). Toronto: University of Toronto Press.

──────────. (1980) *Toronto Workers Respond to Industrial Capitalism, 1867-1892*. Toronto: University of Toronto Press.

──────────. "Joseph C. MacMillan." Biographical note in *Dictionary of Canadian Biography*, Vol. XI, 1881-1890. Toronto: University of Toronto Press.

Kealey, Greg; Palmer, Bryan D. (1982) *Dreaming of what might be: The Knights of Labor in Ontario, 1880-1900*. Cambridge, Mass.: Cambridge University Press.

──────────. (1981) "The Bonds of Unity: The Knights of Labor in Ontario, 1880-1900." *Histoire sociale/Social History*, Vol. XIV, No. 28.

Kealey, Greg; Warrian, Peter, eds. (1976) *Essays in Canadian Working Class History*. Toronto: McClelland and Stewart.

Kennedy, Douglas R. (1956) "The Knights of Labor in Canada." London, Ont.: History of Western Ontario MA thesis.

Kesterton, Wilfred H. (1967) *A History of Journalism in Canada*. Toronto: McClelland and Stewart.

King, Andrew; McCombie, Nick. (1981) "Workers' Comp: Legal Right or Social Welfare." *This Magazine*, Vol. 15, No. 1.

King, William Lyon Mackenzie. (1897) "Trade-Union Organization in the United States." *The Journal of Political Economy* (March).

Knights of Labor (1886) *Proceedings* of the General Assembly, Richmond, VA., Vol. 6.

Landon, Fred. (1942) "The Canadian Scene, 1880-1890." Canadian Historical Association *Report* of the Annual Meeting held at Toronto, May 25-26.

Langdon, Steven. (1975) *The Emergence of the Canadian Working Class Movement, 1845-75*. Toronto: New Hogtown Press.

Laurier, Bruce. (1974) "Nothing on Impulse: Life Styles of Philadelphia Artisans, 1820-1850." *Labor History*, Vol. 15, No. 3.

Laxer, Robert (1976) *Canada's Unions*. Toronto: James Lorimer and Co.

Laxer, Robert, ed. (1973) *Canada Ltd.: The Political Economy of Dependency*. Toronto: McClelland and Stewart.

Lazarus, Morden. (1977) *The Long Winding Road*. Vancouver: Boag Foundation.

──────────. (1977) *Up From the Ranks: Biographical Sketches of 115 Union Leaders*. Toronto: Co-operative Press Associates.

LeBlanc, André Eugene. (1971) "The labour movement seen through the pages of Montreal's *Le Monde Ouvrier/The Labor World*, 1916-1926." Montreal: Université de Montréal Ph.D. thesis.

LeBlanc, André Eugene; Thwaites, James D., eds. (1973) *Le Monde Ouvrier au Québec, bibliographie retrospective*. Montreal: Les presses de l'Université du Québec.

Lennon, Wayne. (1981) "Striking the Balance—The Labour Press and the National Question in Ontario and the Maritimes, 1872-1913." Ottawa: Carleton University MA thesis.

Lipton, Charles. (1967) *The Trade Union Movement in Canada, 1827-1959*. Toronto: New Canada Publications.

Logan, Harold A. (1928) *The History of Trade-Union Organization in Canada*. Chicago: University of Chicago Press.

_____. (1948) *Trade Unions in Canada: Their Development and Functioning*. Toronto: Macmillan.

MacDonald, Joe. (1975) "Robert Drummond, the Provincial Workmen's Association and Political Activity, 1879-1891." Ottawa: Carleton University undergraduate history paper.

MacEwan, Paul. (1976) *Miners and Steelworkers*. Toronto: A.M. Hakkert Ltd.

MacPherson, Ian. (1979) *Each for All: A History of the Co-operative Movement in English Canada*. Toronto: Macmillan.

Masters, Jane Elisabeth. (1970) "Canadian Labour Press Opinion, 1890-1914: A Study in Theoretical Radicalism and Practical Conservatism." London, Ont.: University of Western Ontario MA thesis.

McCabe, D.A.; Lester, R.A. (1938) *Labor and Social Reorganization*. Boston: Little, Brown and Co.

McCormack, A. Ross. (1970) "Arthur Puttee and the Liberal Party, 1899-1904." *Canadian Historical Review*, Vol. LI, No. 2.

_____. (1977) *Reformers, Rebels, and Revolutionaries: The Western Canadian Radical Movement, 1899-1919*. Toronto: University of Toronto Press.

_____. (1978) "British Working-Class Immigrants and Canadian Radicalism: The Case of Arthur Puttee." *Canadian Ethnic Studies*, Vol. X, No. 2.

McGillivray, Derek. (1977) "The Industrial Banner's Views Towards War in 1914." Ottawa: Carleton University MA thesis.

McKay, Ian. (1979) Introduction to C.W. Lunn's *From Trapper Boy to Manager: A Story of Brotherly Love and Perseverance. Labour/Le Travailleur*, Vol. 4.

Middleton, J.E. (1923) *The Municipality of Toronto: A History*. Toronto: Dominion Publishing Co.

Millar, David. (undated) A survey of Canadian labour biographies (Card index compiled by Millar for the committee on Canadian labour history, available at the Canada Labour Library, Hull, Que.)

Morton, Desmond; Copp, Terry. (1980) *Working People: An Illustrated History of Canadian Labour*. Ottawa: Deneau and Greenberg.

Morton, Desmond. (1981) "The Globe and the Labour Question: Ontario Liberalism in the 'Great Upheaval'." *Ontario History*, Vol. LXXIII, No. 1.

Moscovitch, Allan. (1983) *The Welfare State in Canada*. Waterloo, Ont.: Wilfrid Laurier University.

Mott, Frank Luther. (1957) *A History of American Magazines*. Cambridge, Mass.: Harvard University Press.

Moyles, R.G. (1977) *The Blood and Fire in Canada: A History of the Salvation Army in the Dominion, 1882-1976*. Toronto: Peter Martin Associates.

Myers, Gustavus. (1972) *A History of Canadian Wealth*. Toronto: James, Lewis and Samuel.

Naas, B.G.; Sakr, C.S. (1956) *American Labor Union Periodicals: A Guide to Their Location*. Ithica, N.Y.: Cornell University.

Nelles, Viv. (1981) "Rewriting History." *Saturday Night*, February.

Parr, Joy, ed. (1982) *Childhood and Family in Canadian History*. Toronto: McClelland and Stewart.

Parr, Joy. (1980) *Labouring Children: British Immigrant Apprentices to Canada, 1869-1924*. Montreal: McGill-Queen's University Press.

Perline, M.M. (1969) "The Trade Union Press: An Historical Analysis." *Labor History*, Vol. 10, No. 1.

O'Donoghue, Daniel J. (1884-1893) *Labour Organizations in Canada*. Annual reports of the Ontario Bureau of Industries.

Ostry, Bernard. (1960) "Conservatives, Liberals, and Labour in the 1870s." *Canadian Historical Review*, Vol. XLI, No. 1.

——————. (1961) "Conservatives, Liberals, and Labour in the 1880s." *Canadian Journal of Economics and Political Science*, Vol. XXVII, No. 2.

Palmer, Bryan D. (1979) *A Culture in Conflict*. Montreal: McGill-Queen's University Press.

——————. (1983) *Working-Class Experience: The Rise and Reconstruction of Canadian Labour, 1800-1980*. Toronto: Butterworth.

Pentland, H. Clare. (1981) *Labour and Capital in Canada*. Toronto: James Lorimer and Co.

Phillips, Paul. (1967) *No Power Greater: A Century of Labour in B.C.* Vancouver: Boag Foundation/B.C. Federation of Labour.

Raven, Charles E. (1920) *Christian Socialism, 1848-1854*. Toronto: Macmillan.

Reynolds, L.G.; Killingsworth, C.C. (1945) *Trade Union Publications, 1850-1941*. Baltimore: Johns Hopkins Press.

Reilly, Sharon M. (1979) "The Provincial Workmen's Association of Nova Scotia, 1879-1898." Halifax: Dalhousie University MA thesis.

Rice, James R. (1969) "A History of Organized Labour in Saint John, N.B. 1813-1890." Fredericton: University of New Brunswick MA thesis.

Roberts, Wayne. (1976) *Honest Womanhood: Feminism, Femininity and Class Consciousness Among Toronto Working Women, 1896-1914*. Toronto: New Hogtown Press.

Robin, Martin. (1968) *Radical Politics and Canadian Labour*. Kingston, Ont.: Queen's University Industrial Relations Centre.

Rutherford, Paul. (1982) *A Victorian Authority: The Daily Press in Late Nineteenth-Century Canada*. Toronto: University of Toronto Press.

——————. (1978) *The Making of the Canadian Media*. Toronto: McGraw-Hill Ryerson.

——————. (1975) "The People's Press: The Emergence of the New Journalism in Canada, 1869-99." *Canadian Historical Review*, Vol. LVI, No. 2.

Rutherford, Paul, ed. (1974) *Saving the Canadian City: The First Phase, 1880-1920*. Toronto: University of Toronto Press.

Salmon, Edward G. (1886) "What the Working Classes Read." *The Nineteenth Century*, Vol. XX.

Schiller, Dan. (1981) *Objectivity and the News: The Public and the Rise of Commercial Journalism*. Philadelphia: University of Pennsylvania Press.

Schudson, Michael. (1978) *Discovering the News: A Social History of American Newspapers*. New York: Basic Books.

Scotton, Clifford, A. (1956) *A Brief History of Canadian Labor*. Ottawa: Woodsworth House Publishers.

Shedd, F.R.; Odiorne, G.S. (1960) *Political Content of Labor Union Periodicals.* Ann Arbor: Bureau of Industrial Relations, University of Michigan.

Simon, Brian. (1965) *Education and the Labour Movement, 1870-1920.* London: Lawrence and Wishart.

Simpson, James. (undated) Draft autobiography. Available at Baldwin Room, Metropolitan Toronto Library.

Sinclair, Upton. (1920) *The Brass Check.* Pasadena, Calif.: self-published.

––––––––––. (1960) *The Jungle.* New York: Signet/New American Library.

Smart, John David. (1969) "The Patrons of Industry in Ontario." Ottawa: Carleton University MA thesis.

Smith, Anthony. (1980) *Goodbye Gutenberg: The Newspaper Revolution of the 1980s.* New York: Oxford University Press.

Smith, D. Nichol. (undated) "The Newspaper." *Johnson's England.* (city and publisher unknown).

Somers, G.G., ed. (1963) *Labor, Management and Social Policy.* Madison: University of Wisconsin Press.

Sorge, Friedrich A. (1977) *The Labor Movement in the United States, A History of the American Working Class from Colonial Times to 1890.* London: Greenwood Press.

Spector, David. (1975) "The Knights of Labor in Hamilton and Toronto, 1882-1887." Peterborough, Ont.: Trent University MA thesis.

––––––––––. (1975) "The Knights of Labor in Winnipeg, 1883-1891." Winnipeg: University of Winnipeg undergraduate essay.

Splane, Richard B. (1965) *Social Welfare in Ontario, 1791-1893.* Toronto: University of Toronto Press.

Stone, Lawrence. (1964) "The Educational Revolution in England." *Past and Present*, No. 28.

Stunden, Nancy. (1980) "Labour Archives: The Canadian Scene." *International Review on Archives*, Vol. XXVII.

Sutherland, Neil. (1976) *Children in English-Canadian Society: Framing the Twentieth Century Consensus.* Toronto: University of Toronto Press.

Thompson, E.P. (1963) *The Making of the English Working Class.* Harmondsworth, Middlesex, Eng.: Penguin.

Thompson, Lorne. (undated) "The Rise of Labor Unionism in Alberta." Forsey Papers, PAC (MG30 A25, Vol. 12).

Thompson, Thomas Phillips. (1975) *The Politics of Labor.* Toronto: University of Toronto Press.

Wallace, Elisabeth. (1950) "The Origin of the Social Welfare State in Canada, 1867-1900." *Canadian Journal of Economics and Political Science*, Vol. 16, No. 3.

Ware, Norman J. (1959) *The Labor Movement in the United States, 1860-1895: A Study in Democracy.* Gloucester, Mass.: Peter Smith.

––––––––––. (1937) "The History of Labor Interaction." *Labor in Canadian-American Relations.* Toronto: Ryerson Press.

Watt, Frank William. (1957) "Radicalism in English Canadian Literature since Confederation." Toronto: University of Toronto Ph.D. thesis.

Weinrich, Peter. (1982) *Social Protest from the Left in Canada, 1870-1970: A Bibliography.* Toronto: University of Toronto Press.

Williams, Jack. (1975) *The Story of Unions in Canada*. Toronto: J.M. Dent and Sons.

Wismer, Leslie E. (1951) *Canadian Labor Union*. Proceedings of the congresses. Ottawa: Trades and Labour Congress of Canada.

——————. (1951) *Workers Way to a Fair Share*. Ottawa: Trades and Labour Congress of Canada.

Wolseley, R.E.; Campbell, L.R. (1949) *Exploring Journalism*. New York: Prentice-Hall.

Wood, Aubrey. (1975) *A History of Farmers' Movements in Canada*. Toronto: University of Toronto Press.

Woodworth, A.V. (1903) *Christian Socialism in England*. London: Swan Sonnenschein and Co.

Woodsworth, J.S. (1972) *My Neighbour*. Toronto: University of Toronto Press.

Woolley, J.G.; Johnson, W.E. (1903) *Temperance Progress of the Century*. London: Linscott Publishing Co.

Wrigley, G. Weston. (1901) "Socialism in Canada." *International Socialist Review*. London: Vol. 1, May.

Wylie, Robin. (undated) "The Political Economy of 19th-Century Working-Class Struggle: Canada's Nine-Hour Men and the Practice of Commodity Fetishism." Ottawa: Carleton University history essay.

Ziegler, Phil. (1969) "Appendix II—A Symposium on the Labor Press." *American Labor Dynamics*. New York: Arno and *The New York Times*.

Zwerker, Sally. (1982) *The Rise and Fall of the Toronto Typographical Union, 1832-1972—A Case Study of Foreign Domination*. Toronto: University of Toronto Press.

Index

D

Daily City News, 74
Daily Clarion, 122
Daily Herald, 58
Daily Worker, 122
Debs, Eugene V., 104
DeLeon, Daniel, 114
Detroit Free Press, 51
Dickens, Charles, 80
direct legislation, 78
Direct Legislation League of
    Canada, 114
Donavon, Eugene, 47-57, 65
Doukhobors, 117
Drummond, Robert, 35-50
dual unionism, 80
Dunkin Act (1854), 15

E

Eagle, (Ferguson, then
    Lardeau, B.C.) 118
early shop closings movement,
    23, 99
Eastern Federationist, 122
Eastern Labour News, 122
Echo, 81, 83-90, 96
Edmonton Free Press, 122
education, 56, 23-24, 28, 37,
    40, 56-57, 77, 84, 87, 103,
    105-106, 115, 129
eight-hour day movement, 93,
    101, 105
Election News, 13
Elizabethan Poor Laws, 8
employer liability acts, 49, 65
Engels, Frederick, 29
Enjolras, 52, 74, 86-87
Equalizer (Brockville, Ont.), 128
Evening News (Toronto), 97
Evening News (London), 128
Evening Palladium, 58
Evening Star (Toronto), 97
Evening Traveller (Boston), 74

F

factory acts, 49, 89
Fahey, James A., 22
family allowances, 108
Family Compact, 13
Fenian Raids, 74
Fielding, (Premier W.S.), 43, 45
Fincher's Trade Review, 7, 23
Finlay, Hugh, 36
First World War, 98, 119, 122
Fisherman (Vancouver), ix, 126
Foreman, T.A., 105, 116
Franklin, Benjamin, 5
Fraser, John (Cousin Sandy),
    29
Free Lance (Ottawa), 96-97, 128

G

Gazette (Halifax), 5
George, Henry, 48, 74, 114
Globe, 19, 26, 31, 67-68, 74, 95;
    Globe and Mail, xi, 127
Gompers, Samuel, 104
Goodwin's, 131
government-assisted immigra-
    tion, 27, 49, 57, 65, 84-85
Grand Trunk Railway, 91
Great Unstamped, 2
Grip, 68, 80, 116
Grip Printing and Publishing
    Company, 80
Grits, 21, 24, 47
Gronlund, Laurence, 74, 114
Guardian (New York), 127
Guelph Herald, 63

H

Halifax Chronicle, 45
Halifax Herald, 45
Hambling, Skip, 124, 126
Hamilton Board of Trade, 12
Hamilton Co-operative
    Association, 16

Hamilton Trades and Labour
Council, 96
Hardie, James Keir, 98
Harvey, Falconer L., 58
Haymarket Riot, 56
health care, 39, 40, 116
Herald (Montreal), 83
Hind, Cora D., 101
Hislop, Charles, 104
Hislop, Mrs. Charles, 101
Holland, Dr. J.G., 42
Horsiot, Cyrille, 86, 89
housing, 40, 77, 87, 93, 102,
116, 129
Houston, John, 122
Howe, Joseph, 3, 36, 46
Howell, George A., 76
Howland, (Toronto Mayor)
W.H., 61
Hudson Bay Company, 3
Hugo, Victor, 52

I

illiteracy, 5-6, 28
Independent (Bobcaygeon,
Ont.), 67
Independent (Vancouver), 103
Independent Labour Party
(Winnipeg), 107
Indicator (Vancouver), 122
Industrial Banner, 81, 90-98,
112, 116, 122; Hamilton
edition, 96;
Toronto edition, 97
Industrial Brotherhood of
Canada, 91
Industrial News (Winnipeg), 99
Industrial Relations Commis-
sion (B.C.), 131
Industrial Workers of the
World, 108, 118
Industrial World (Rossland,
B.C.), 118
Ingram, A.B., 70, 112

International Typographical
Union, 100, 105; Local 85,
36, 96
In These Times, 127
Ivens, William, 122

J

Japanese immigration, 117, 129
Johnson, Dr. Samuel, 5
Journal and Pictou News
(Stellarton, N.S.), 45
Journal of Industry, 13
Journal of United Labour, 71
Justice, 58

K

Kansas City New Argo, 57
Kilt, J.G., 96-97, 113
King, William Lyon Mackenzie,
81, 104
Kingsmill, R., 62
Knights of Labour, 32, 46-52,
56, 58-81, 83, 87, 91, 95, 97,
99, 102, 112-113; District
Assembly 61, 71; District
Assembly 125, 71, 75;
District Assembly 138, 91;
Local Assembly 119, 47;
Local Assembly 7814, 75;
Local Assembly 7110, 91

L

Labour Advocate, 73-81, 83, 90,
96, 128
labour candidates, 30, 43-44,
54, 56, 64, 78, 94
Labour Day, 83, 100, 128
Labour Educational Associa-
tion, 91, 98
Labour Educational Publishing
Company, 97
Labour Gazette, 81, 104
Labour News (Hamilton), 122
Labour News, 124

W

Wage-Earner (Ottawa), 96
Wage-Worker, 50, 128
Wallaceburg Record, 112
War of 1812, 3
Watts, Charles, 69
Wayland, J.A., 93
Week, 66-67
Weekly News (Halifax), 96
Weekly Sun, 97, 113
Weekly Toiler (Saint John, N.B.),
  96
Western Clarion, 119, 122
Western Federation of Miners,
  118
Western Labour News, 122
Western Socialist, 119
Western Workman, 22
Whigs, 9, 68
Wilkes, John, 2
Williams, James S., 9, 19-32, 40
Winnipeg Board of Control,
  108
Winnipeg Free Press, 103, 105
Winnipeg General Strike, 119,
  122
Winnipeg Industrial News, 66
Winnipeg Trades and Labour
  Council, 100

Winnipeg Typographer, 100
Winnipeg Typographical Union
  (Local 191), 105
Woman's Labour League, 106
woman's rights, 26, 41, 48, 51,
  55, 65, 76, 83, 87-89, 93, 101,
  106, 114-115, 117
woman beating, 65
Woodsworth, J.S., 131
Worker (Toronto), 96
Working Man's Advocate, 7
Workingman's Advocate
  (Chicago), 30
*Workingman's Friend and Political
  Magazine*, 1
Workingman's Journal, 17, 22,
  32, 37, 50, 63, 86, 121
Working Man's Party (United
  States), 7
Workman (Saint John, N.B.), 96
worker's compensation, 39, 108
Worker's Weekly, 122
workplace health and safety,
  26, 39, 65, 77, 116, 129
Wright, Alexander Whyte, xiii,
  62-66, 70-71
Wrigley, George, 61, 69-71, 97,
  111-119, 122, 128
Wrigley, G. Weston, 111